Trust

No

One

FEDERAL BUREAU OF INVESTIGATION

Date 1 April 1979

Field Report

March 30, 1979

Following relocation from Martha's Vineyard to Washington, DC, BILL MULDER and his son are under surveillance to ensure compliance. Mulder's work on ▮▮▮▮▮▮▮▮▮▮▮▮▮ is critical at this time. Work at SD, HQ, Pentagon and ▮▮▮▮▮▮ location.

SUBJ FOX WILLIAM MULDER, 17 years of age, exhibits a photographic memory and a high level of intelligence. He has NBC as to the circumstances around ▮▮▮▮▮▮▮ ▮▮▮▮▮▮'s disappearance—agent may ▮▮▮▮▮▮▮▮▮ to keep him in the dark SYD. Evaluate for future recruitment for ▮▮▮▮▮▮ within SD.

Also watch his relationship with ▮▮▮▮▮▮▮▮; father ▮▮▮▮▮▮▮▮ ▮▮▮▮▮▮ worked at ▮▮▮▮ Air Force Base. Wife was ▮▮▮▮▮▮▮▮▮ ▮▮▮▮

Wife/mother TEENA MULDER remains in the family home and is not under surveillance.
—X

Field Report

April 1, 1979

CAPTAIN SCULLY recently relocated the family from Miramar Naval Base back to Annapolis, MD. Promotion to Admiral discussed. Transfer was initiated by ▮▮▮▮▮▮. Youngest child SUBJ DANA KATHERINE, born February 23, 1964. ▮▮▮▮▮ vaccination 29510 on ▮▮▮▮▮▮▮▮▮.

Aged 15 years, subject shows signs of seeing ▮▮▮▮▮▮▮▮▮▮▮ and/or post death. Bears observation and testing R&I. Such ▮▮▮▮ may help departments communicate with the ▮▮▮▮ we have entered into a treaty with October 13, 1973, ▮▮▮▮ Air Force Base.

Continue surveillance. Test with ▮▮▮▮▮ protocol.
—SA Gerlich

On __1 April 1979__ At ____DC/Maryland____ File # _____

By Special Agents _____X_____ Date Dictated_____

THE X FILES
ORIGINS

AGENT OF CHAOS

Kami Garcia

{Imprint}
MAKE YOUR MARK
New York

[Imprint]
MAKE YOUR MARK

A part of Macmillan Children's Publishing Group,
a division of Macmillan Publishing Group, LLC

THE X-FILES ORIGINS: AGENT OF CHAOS. The X-Files ™ & © 2017 Twentieth
Century Fox Film Corporation. All rights reserved. Printed in the United
States of America by LSC Communications US, LLC (Lakeside Classic),
Harrisonburg, Virginia. For information, address Imprint, 175 Fifth Avenue,
New York, N.Y. 10010.

Library of Congress Cataloging-in-Publication Data is available.

ISBN 978-1-250-11956-8 (hardcover) / ISBN 978-1-250-11957-5 (ebook)

Our books may be purchased in bulk for promotional, educational, or business use. Please contact your local bookseller or the Macmillan Corporate
and Premium Sales Department at (800) 221-7945 ext. 5442 or by e-mail at
MacmillanSpecialMarkets@macmillan.com.

Book design by Ellen Duda

Imprint logo designed by Amanda Spielman

First Edition—2017

1 3 5 7 9 10 8 6 4 2

fiercereads.com

If you steal this book, they will find you. It's a global conspiracy, actually,
with key players in the highest level of power that reaches down into the lives
of every man, woman, and child on this planet.

For Stella, Nick, and Alex

I hope you never stop believing.

For Erin Stein and Derek Racca

You're true believers. Leave a trail of
sunflower seeds for the rest of us to follow.

We work in the dark. We do what we can to battle the evil that would otherwise destroy us. But if a man's character is his fate, this fight is not a choice but a calling. Yet sometimes the weight of this burden causes us to falter, breaching the fragile fortress of our mind, allowing the monsters without to turn within. We are left alone staring into the abyss, into the laughing face of madness.

—Fox Mulder, *The X-Files*

CHAPTER 1

Washington, DC
March 30, 1979, 3:32 P.M.

Packs of teenagers, pumped for the official start of spring break,
rushed past the black sedan parked across from the high school,
unaware they were being watched from behind the car's tinted
windows. Jocks wearing Wilson High jerseys carried pretty cheer-
leaders on their shoulders, enjoying the chance to finally touch some
thigh. Other guys horsed around in the road, showing off for girls
in tight jeans who pretended not to notice them.

Most of the teens didn't give the car a second glance. Black
vehicles with tinted windows were as common as pigeons in
Washington, DC—home base of the Secret Service, the CIA, and
the FBI.

The man in the passenger seat scanned the face of every boy

jaywalking across the road, searching for one in particular. "No sign of him yet," he said, directing his comment at the older man behind the wheel.

"A powerful observation, Reginald," his boss deadpanned. He sounded like somebody's grandfather, and next to Reggie, he looked like one.

Reggie's dark brown skin was as smooth as a newborn baby's, and the short Afro tucked under his tweed newsboy cap only added to his boyish good looks. His bushy black mustache and sophisticated style—like the fitted white shirt, tan suede blazer, and flared black slacks he had on today—kept him from being mistaken for a college kid.

Even if the boss ditched the starched shirt, wide tie, and conservative side part, he couldn't hide the lines etched into his pale skin like scars, or the worn look behind his cold eyes.

Reggie turned his attention back to the teens. They were still running on adrenaline and the illusion of freedom that youth offered. He watched them with a pang of envy. "It's like they think nothing can touch them. Remember how that felt?"

"No. I was never an idiot." The boss tapped his thumb against the steering wheel without disturbing the funnel of ash on the end of the cigarette in his hand. "People see what they want to see, which is generally nothing important."

So much for small talk, Reggie thought as he continued to search the horde of kids. "There's no way we could've missed him."

"Your powers of deduction never disappoint me." The boss took a drag from the Morley and exhaled slowly.

The cloud of smoke made Reggie's eyes water, but he ignored it and focused on the funnel of ash, waiting for it to break off.

"The prodigal son appears." The boss pointed his cigarette across the street at two boys walking down the sidewalk with backpacks slung over their shoulders.

Fox Mulder was a handsome kid—lean like a swimmer, with a look that was the perfect balance between clean-cut and I-don't-give-a-crap. His dark brown hair hit just past the collar of his striped shirt, and the front was long enough to cover his eyes a little. Girls ate up that kind of thing. Fox stared into space as he shuffled along, holding a crumpled piece of paper.

The other boy was a different story. He was shorter than Fox by a foot, and the kid's straight blond hair hung in his face, as if he was growing out a bad bowl haircut. His dirt-brown T-shirt featured a faded image of a scene from *Star Wars*, and his jeans were so long that the frayed bottoms dragged on the sidewalk.

The kid was talking nonstop, gesturing wildly and buzzing around Fox like a housefly. From the look of it, he could use a strip of duct tape to cover his mouth.

Reggie wasn't a fan of talkers. They were a liability. "Who's the kid with Bill Mulder's son?"

"Are you familiar with the concept of research?" The boss finally tapped the cigarette against the edge of the ashtray, and the ash broke off in one piece, as if on command. He crushed the butt and focused his watery-blue eyes on Reggie. "Let me enlighten you. It's a practice professionals use to obtain information so we don't have to rely on *assumptions*."

Reggie was tempted to fire back with a smart remark of his own, but the boss would make him regret it later. The organization they worked for was built on the backs of men and women with ice running through their veins—individuals willing to do whatever needed to be done, regardless of the cost—and the smoking man next to him was one of them.

"What's my assignment?" Reggie wanted to get down to business. "Do you want me to collect Bill's son?"

Collect sounded more civilized than *abduct*.

"Taking Samantha Mulder was partly insurance to keep her father from talking." The boss opened a new pack of cigarettes and flicked his wrist, freeing one from the box. "And we all had to make sacrifices. But it would break Bill if we took his son, too, and right now we need him. The Project is at a critical stage that requires people with specific skills, and Bill Mulder is one of them."

He lit the Morley and continued talking, with the cigarette tucked in the corner of his mouth. "So we have to keep an eye on Bill and his son. Follow the boy around and let me know if he does anything interesting. We're also assessing Fox for potential recruitment."

Tailing a teenager during spring break was a crap job, but

Reggie wasn't high enough in the food chain yet to complain about it. Instead he asked, "Who the hell names their kid Fox? His parents must hate him."

"Bill and Teena are too busy hating each other. They were barely speaking when Bill moved out of the house in the fall." The boss stared out the window, tracking Fox Mulder's progress down the street. "The timing was perfect, actually. We stepped in and relocated Bill from Martha's Vineyard to DC so he could work on the Project full-time. Fox came with him."

"I'm surprised the kid's mom let him go," Reggie said. "My aunt and uncle divorced when I was young, and they butted heads about everything."

"If I gave you the impression that I want to swap childhood memories, let me clarify. I don't." He took a long drag from his cigarette, and a new funnel of ash began to form. "Interestingly enough, sending Fox to live with his dad was Teena's idea."

"Doesn't that seem strange?" Reggie asked, ignoring the insult.

"It does." The boss exhaled, and a ribbon of smoke curled its way toward Reggie, who finally coughed and reached for the window handle. The boss snapped his fingers and pointed at the glass. "It stays up."

Reggie ignored the burning sensation in his throat. He refused to appear weak in front of a man who had once referred to weakness as a disease during a debriefing. "Do you think Fox's mom knows something?"

"The jury is still out. But when the verdict comes in, I'll deal with Teena Mulder personally." Another trail of smoke snaked from the boss's chapped lips. "You focus on Fox. Update me directly—and only me."

"So no reports?"

"Keep them to a minimum. We don't want to leave any bread crumbs. So from this point on, you no longer have a name.

"Sign your reports as 'X.'"

CHAPTER 2

Fox Mulder stared at the *C* written at the top of his history test as he walked down the sidewalk with Gimble. His friend hadn't stopped talking since the bell rang at the end of sixth period, officially signaling the beginning of spring break. That was the thing about Gimble—nothing fazed the guy. He would never waste his time worrying about one lousy grade, but Mulder couldn't let it go.

After three tests that had all followed the same format—thirty multiple-choice questions taken directly from the textbook and twenty short-answer questions—their history teacher had thrown the class a curveball and switched to essay questions.

"I don't get it." Gimble glanced at Mulder's paper. "Didn't you read the chapters?"

"Yeah."

"Then what gives?" Gimble asked. "With that superpower of yours, you should've aced the test."

"A photographic memory isn't a superpower. It's an anomaly." *And a social curse*, Mulder thought.

The fact that Mulder could remember every word he read annoyed people at school—his classmates, because even if they spent days studying for a test, Mulder would still score higher; and his teachers, because they hated the fact that he knew more than they did.

So Mulder didn't tell anyone about his memory if he could avoid it. But it was hard to hide from Gimble once they became friends. After Mulder quoted whole pages from *Starlog* magazine, word for word, he gave himself away.

But his photographic memory couldn't have helped him today. Mulder crumpled up the test and stuffed it in the back pocket of his jeans.

Gimble noticed and seemed to take it as a sign that Mulder was stressed about his grade. "Maybe it was just an off day and your circuitry got crossed?"

"I don't have off days." *At least not because of my memory*, Mulder thought. "That's not the way it works. I remember everything from the reading."

"Then how did you end up with a C?"

"American history textbooks are biased," Mulder said. "Lots of information in them is inaccurate."

Gimble smacked a palm against his forehead. "Dude? Tell me you didn't write that on the test?"

"When did the delegates of the Continental Congress sign the Declaration of Independence?" Mulder asked without missing a beat. "Give me a date."

"This is obviously a trick question." Gimble frowned, concentrating. "We're talking about *the* Declaration of Independence— the one signed by fifty-six men, with John Hancock's famous signature on it?"

"That's the one."

"Easy. July fourth, 1776," Gimble said confidently.

"Don't try out for *Jeopardy!* anytime soon, because you are incorrect," Mulder said. "The Continental Congress voted for independence on July second. July fourth is the date the Declaration was *adopted* by the Congress and signed by John Hancock."

"How is that any different from what I said? You asked when the delegates *signed*, not when they *voted*."

Mulder nodded. "True. But Hancock was the only delegate who signed on July fourth."

"Now you're just messing with me." Gimble wasn't buying it. "I've seen the real Declaration of Independence, at the National Archives. The bottom is covered with signatures."

"Fifty-six," Mulder said. "And most of them signed on August second. Look it up—just not in our history textbook."

Gimble scratched his head. "Our book sucks. I get it. But why didn't you just write down whatever it says and walk away with an A?"

Mulder shrugged. "Because the information is wrong."

"Who cares?"

I do.

Mulder was sick of people feeding him lies. He had to choke them down at home, but he refused to do it at school, too.

"Will your dad be pissed about your grade?" Gimble asked.

Mulder snorted. "He doesn't even know I had a test."

"You're lucky. The Major is always asking me questions. I wouldn't be surprised if he had a copy of the class syllabus."

He'd never met Gimble's dad, but from what his friend had told him, the man sounded intense. Most fathers wouldn't make their sons call them "the Major."

"Your dad can't be that bad," Mulder said. "Not many people have a wide-field reflecting telescope at home."

Gimble grinned. "Okay . . . the telescope *is* pretty rad. A friend of the Major's from the air force got ahold of it for him. It's nothing like the amateur-grade models they sell in stores."

"Seriously? I had no idea." Mulder laid on the sarcasm. "I'm completely unfamiliar with Newtonian infinite-axis telescopes."

"Show-off."

Mulder laughed. "It would be nice to put my insomnia to good use and get an asteroid or Martian crater named after me like George Hale. Are you sure your dad won't mind if I try it out?"

"I told you he said it was cool." Gimble flicked his head to the side just enough to get the long hair out of his eyes—something he did at least fifty times a day. "Let's go see a guy about a telescope."

Mulder picked up his pace. As a kid, he'd wanted to be an astronaut when he grew up. He was ten years old when his dad told him that it would never happen. Astronauts had to pass a vision test, and Mulder had protanopia—a type of red-green color-blindness. Most people thought it meant that he couldn't distinguish between red and green, but protanopia only affected his ability to see red. One color. That was all it took to crush Mulder's dream.

"There's a bunch of other stuff I want to show you, too." Gimble scrambled ahead and turned around to walk backward, facing Mulder. "I've got forty-eight *Star Trek* cards, not including doubles. No one counts doubles, you know? And I have the Dr. 'Bones' McCoy card that came out three years ago, in mint condition."

"That's cool." Mulder was used to epic levels of *Star Trek* devotion. Phoebe, his best friend back home in Martha's Vineyard, collected the trading cards, too, along with everything else related to the TV show or the movie.

"I've got something even cooler." Gimble stumbled on a crack in the pavement but managed to catch himself. "Well, maybe not *cooler*, but almost as cool. Or equally as cool," he said, as if the *Star Trek* gods had tripped him for making the comment.

"Like what?"

Gimble turned onto a residential street lined with brownstones. Instead of answering the question, he stopped in front of the second house. "This is it."

"I hope you have good junk food." Mulder followed his friend up the steps. "All we have at my dad's is sunflower seeds."

Gimble hesitated at the door. "The Major is kind of strange. I told you that, right?"

"At least a hundred times," Mulder said. "Including thirty seconds ago. Whose dad isn't?"

"'Kind of' is probably an understatement. And all the news reports about that missing kid are making him worse."

Billy Christian—that was the little boy's name.

For a moment, Mulder couldn't catch his breath. It felt like someone was squeezing all the air out of his lungs, and then the feeling passed, like it always did. Gimble was still talking. "My mom's death really screwed him up, you know?"

"I get it." Mulder's mother had never been the same after his younger sister, Samantha, disappeared almost five and a half years ago. Every night she would put on her apron and prepare one of her specialties—meat loaf or a casserole—in an attempt to make it feel as if their family wasn't falling apart. She would sit at the kitchen table and read a magazine or clip coupons while she waited for the oven timer to go off. After the third time he found his mom staring into space, while the oven timer buzzed and a casserole burned to a crisp in the oven ten feet away from her, Mulder learned to listen for the buzzer.

One night, he made the mistake of taking a shower before it went off. By the time he made it to the kitchen, the alarm was blaring and a veil of black smoke had filled the kitchen. His mom sat in the midst of it all, her cheeks smudged with tears.

Mulder swallowed hard and pushed away the memory. "Are we going inside or what?"

"I guess." Gimble took out his keys and unlocked the five dead bolts on the door.

Mulder followed him inside, but he stopped cold just past the front hallway. It opened up into what Mulder assumed was supposed to be the living room, but he wasn't sure because every square inch of the space—except for a sofa, a recliner, and a small patch of shag carpet in the center—was covered with junk.

No wonder Gimble hadn't invited him over before. Most people would've taken off the moment they walked in, but Mulder found his friend's house oddly fascinating.

"The Major saves everything." Gimble walked over to the television set and picked up a two-way radio sitting on top. He pressed the button on the side and spoke into it. "It's me. I'm home."

Static crackled through the speaker, followed by a man's gravelly voice. "This is a secure line. Code words?"

Gimble rolled his eyes. "Agent of Chaos."

The radio crackled again. "Meet me at the extraction point at sixteen hundred."

"He means four o'clock," Gimble explained to Mulder before signing off. "Got it. I'm out." He returned the two-way radio to its original location on top of the TV set, his shoulders sagging. "Sorry. If I don't 'report in' when I get home, the Major will think I'm an intruder."

"That could be interesting." Mulder grinned to let Gimble know that he wasn't judging.

Gimble perked up. "You don't want to be the guinea pig in that experiment. Trust me."

Mulder thought the whole code word thing was sort of cool, like everything else in the room. But dropping by after school wasn't the same as living here. He took a closer look around.

In addition to books, a row of bookshelves held small cardboard boxes with masking tape labels, numbered VHS tapes, two shortwave radios, some kind of handheld transceiver or CB, a sextant, bowls of rocks, and boxes of cream-filled snack cakes. Mulder picked up a gray rock the size of his fist and tossed it in his hand like a baseball. Nothing special about it, as far as he could tell.

He moved on to the books, scanning the titles in some of the stacks: *The Encyclopedia of Unexplained Phenomena*, *Breaking the Crop Circle Code*, *Evolution and the Human Brain*, *The Truth About Abraham Lincoln's Assassination*, *Secrets of the Solar System*, and *Applied Astrophysics*. There were a few titles he recognized—like

The Hitchhiker's Guide to the Galaxy, 1984, and *The Martian Chronicles*—and at least half a dozen paperback copies of a book Mulder had never heard of called *Stormbringer.* Judging by the long-haired albino warrior on the cover, it was a fantasy novel.

The room was jam-packed, but Mulder realized the Major had created his own organizational system. Newspapers and magazines were stacked against the walls according to publication and year, and the towers of books beside them were sorted by category, like physics, space exploration, natural disasters, American presidents, and . . . aliens?

But the Major's taste in reading material wasn't nearly as interesting as the wallpaper job he'd given the room. Newspaper clippings and photos of what resembled crop circles and UFOs obscured most of the blue paint, and a huge map covered the far wall, with pieces of yellow string crisscrossing between the colored pushpins.

"What is all this?" Mulder stared at the walls, transfixed.

"The Major is always tracking something—natural disasters, meteors, unusual weather patterns, shortwave radio transmissions. You name it." Gimble's cheeks turned red and he looked away. "Let's head to my room before he comes up from the basement. That's where he keeps his files."

"What kind of files?" After seeing the walls, Mulder was curious.

"Who knows? Maybe he's saving the 'secret messages' he

decodes from the backs of our cereal boxes." Gimble kept his tone light as he led Mulder through the kitchen to a back staircase. He sounded worn out and kind of embarrassed, so Mulder pretended not to notice a bicycle lock wrapped around the refrigerator door handles.

Gimble's bedroom was at the top of the steps.

"This is it," his friend said proudly as he opened the door.

When Mulder walked in, his first thought was how much Gimble's bedroom reminded him of Phoebe's. Books overflowed the shelves, and a miniature model of the *Enterprise* hung above a small desk. Handwritten lists and charts were taped on a wall next to a *Star Wars* movie poster that still had fold marks on it.

Another poster covered the back of Gimble's door—Farrah Fawcett, wearing the red bathing suit that sent every girl at school to the mall to buy a red one-piece. Mulder had the same poster on his bedroom wall back home.

He pointed to Farrah. "Now I know why we get along."

"Think she's a Trekkie?" Gimble asked hopefully.

"Doubt it." Mulder took a closer look at the miniature *Enterprise*. The model was meticulously hand-painted just like Phoebe's, though Gimble had added a white *G* on the back of his ship.

Gimble sighed, still checking out Farrah. "You're probably right. Nobody's perfect."

Farrah Fawcett is pretty close.

"Wait till you see this." Gimble rushed to his nightstand and opened the drawer. He turned around slowly with one hand behind his back, and then made a dramatic show of revealing what he was holding.

A pamphlet.

"It's an original zine from Lord Manhammer."

Mulder shrugged. "Am I supposed to know who that is?"

"Have I taught you *nothing* in the past three months? Lord Manhammer . . . the king of D and D?"

"Dungeons and Dragons?" Mulder asked. Most of what he knew about the role-playing game he'd learned from listening to Gimble talk about it. Even Gimble's nickname—which everyone, including the teachers, called him—came straight out of the game.

"There's only one D and D."

"Not true," Mulder said. "There's drunk and disorderly and deuterium deuterium."

"How could I forget deuterium deuterium?" Gimble groaned with an exaggerated head smack. "When most people hear 'D and D,' their minds *definitely* go straight to nuclear fusion." He held up the pamphlet, undeterred. "This is a copy of *Lord Manhammer's Underground EP Strategy Guide*. It outlines Manhammer's strategy for accumulating experience points. He only printed four hundred copies, and I have one of them."

"Can I take a look?" Mulder asked. Gimble was his only real

friend in DC. The least he could do was fake a little interest in what seemed like his prized possession.

Gimble handed him the newsprint pamphlet. "Be careful. The paper is thin."

Mulder took it and thumbed through the pages. Lots of references to *armor class* and *adventure goals*. Serious geek stuff. Phoebe would love it.

"Interesting, huh?" Gimble craned his neck to see which page Mulder was reading. "We have an empty spot in our party."

"D and D isn't really my thing. I played once, and I sucked." Mulder handed him back the pamphlet.

"At least give it some thought. Our dungeon master, Theo, likes new blood, and you've got me. I'm the best teacher around."

"I'll think about it." *Then I'll say no.*

Gimble returned Lord Manhammer's sacred text to the nightstand. "Want to take a look at my *Star Trek* cards before we check out the telescope? It'll give you something to talk about if you get stuck meeting the Major later—which you probably will—since he watches *Project U.F.O.* in the living room every day at four."

"The show about aliens?" Mulder had watched a few episodes with Phoebe.

"More like the people who believe in them."

"I didn't know it was on every day."

"It's not," Gimble said. "We have it on VHS. The Major tapes the episodes and watches one every day at four, even on Christmas Day. He usually makes me watch it with him."

Mulder tried to imagine his dad videotaping a show for them to watch together. But it was too hard, because it would never happen.

"It's actually a decent show if you want to watch a little," Gimble offered. "Some of the UFO footage looks real."

"Maybe it is. NASA's Ames Research Center still hasn't found a way to explain the Wow! signal."

"Funny." Gimble flicked his head to the side to get the hair out of his eyes. "Don't say anything like that around the Major. He's crazy enough without any encouragement."

"Has he always been like that?"

"No. It started right after my mom died. Her car went off the side of a bridge. The Major couldn't handle losing her. He retraced every move she made that day. He ate bran flakes for breakfast just like she had that morning. He scrubbed the bathtub and wore her flowered rubber gloves when he washed the dishes. He even found the fantasy novel she'd been reading on her nightstand—*Stormbringer*—and he read it cover to cover. That's where the Major got the idea for the code words—Agent of Chaos." Gimble took an octagonal die he used in D & D games out of his pocket and rolled it between his fingers nervously. "That's when he started talking about Chaos and Law, government conspiracies, and collateral damage. Someone on the base must've found out about it, because he was discharged right after that."

"Sorry, man. I didn't know."

Gimble shrugged. "Nobody does. It's the kind of thing you keep to yourself."

Mulder knew how it felt to keep secrets about your life. He hadn't told Gimble about his sister—or even mentioned that he had one. Transferring to a new school for senior year gave Mulder a chance to walk through the halls with people who didn't know the story that plagued him back home.

When Samantha disappeared, everyone on the island heard the same version of events. One minute his sister was watching television in the living room with Mulder . . . and the next minute she was gone. He was there the whole time, so why couldn't he remember anything? That was the first question people asked. Overnight, he became the poor kid who froze when his little sister needed him.

The police and the FBI never recovered any evidence to explain Samantha's disappearance. Mulder believed she'd been kidnapped, but no one took him seriously. Why should they when his father refused to acknowledge the possibility?

Instead, Bill Mulder sent his son to a shrink. Mulder's parents never used the word *kidnapped*, at least not around him. They saved it for the endless arguments they had in their bedroom at night, when they thought he was asleep. But Mulder rarely slept.

He spent his nights lying awake, making a silent vow. If the authorities refused to figure out what happened to his sister, he would do it himself.

"Mulder? You okay?" Gimble was waving his hand in front of Mulder's face.

"Yeah. Sorry. I didn't sleep much last night." He fake-yawned.

"Gary? Are you coming down?" the Major called from downstairs. "It's almost sixteen hundred."

"I'll be down in a minute," Gimble yelled, red-faced.

"Gary?" Mulder grinned. "That's your real name?"

"No one calls me that except my father. Gimble is my true name. And I don't make fun of your name, *Fox*."

"Hey, I'm not judging." Mulder held up his hands in surrender. "As long as I don't have to call you Lord Manhammer."

When they reached the staircase, the Major was stationed at the bottom, waiting. He had the tired look of a man who had fought too many battles. Deep lines were etched into his face, and his standard military-style buzz cut was uneven, as if it had been trimmed by a shaky hand. The Major was dressed in freshly ironed olive green fatigues. The button-down shirt hung from his tall frame, too tight in some places and too loose in others. It looked like a real military uniform—complete with a blue air force patch sewn above one pocket and *Winchester*, his last name, sewn above the other pocket. There were other patches, too, stars and a fancy crest with gold wings on the sides.

Gimble leaned toward Mulder and whispered, "Whatever you do, just don't tell him that your dad works for the government."

"Why not?" Fox glanced at the intimidating man staring up at him.

"You don't want to know."

CHAPTER 3

Winchester Residence
3:56 P.M.

The Major extended his hand before Mulder made it down the steps. "Major William Wyatt Winchester, United States Air Force, 128th Reconnaissance Squadron."

Mulder stuck out his sweaty palm. "Fox Mulder. Gim—I mean, Gary's friend from school."

The Major clasped his hand in a death grip and shook it. "Gary tells me you have security clearance?"

Security clearance?

Mulder's dad tossed around the term all the time in an attempt to make his boring job at the State Department sound interesting. Mulder wasn't sure the Major had enough clearance to get into his own bank account.

Gimble did a face-palm, Mulder's cue to play along. "Of course, sir."

The Major nodded and headed for the living room, motioning for the boys to follow him. "Glad to hear it. I can never be too careful. My work is highly classified, and the government would kill to get their hands on it." He gestured at the sofa and turned on the TV set and the VHS player. "Have a seat."

"If you don't mind me asking, what's *your* clearance level?" After seeing the house, Mulder couldn't resist asking.

Gimble's eyes bugged out, and he mouthed, *What the hell?*

The Major laughed. "This is a black op, son, and it's my operation. Clearance doesn't get much higher than that. Every move I make is classified." He tapped on an AM radio on the shelf above the VHS player. "All my communications are encrypted, and information is supplied on a need-to-know basis."

"Which means no one knows anything," Gimble said under his breath.

"How many people are in your unit?" Mulder asked.

And are they real?

If the Major knew that Mulder was humoring him, he didn't let on. "I keep my unit small—three people, including myself. The members of my unit are true patriots, willing to risk their lives to expose a government conspiracy of epic proportions."

"I'm going to show Mulder the telescope," Gimble said.

"You're not going to watch the transmission?" the Major asked.

"I'll watch *Project U.F.O.* with you tomorrow. Mulder wants to see the telescope. He's into space stuff."

"We can check it out after the episode," Mulder offered, sitting on the shag carpet. "I don't mind."

The Major nodded his approval. "That's what I like to hear."

"Fine." Gimble looked annoyed. "Then can we start watching it?"

The Major crossed his arms. "I don't think I heard you correctly, airman."

Gimble stood and saluted his father. "Can we start watching it, *sir*!"

As if on cue, the opening sequence filled the TV screen and the Major sat down in his recliner. Mulder was sucked in the moment the opening montage started. Diagrams of schematics of flying saucers straight out of a sci-fi novel filled the screen, while a narrator explained that biblical Ezekiel "saw the wheel"—a UFO—and other people have seen them, too. So the US Air Force created a team to investigate.

"Of course they chose *our* boys," the Major said, touching the US Air Force patch on his chest. "But they never wanted them to actually find anything."

The episode dramatized a scout leader's encounter with a UFO, outside a small Mississippi town. "I saw a flash of light in the sky, and I went to check it out."

A fake UFO that looked like a spaceship in a comic book zapped the guy with lasers that left his arm covered in burns.

"It was probably swamp gas playing tricks on the guy, like they said at the beginning," Gimble said.

"That's what the government wants you to believe." The Major was glued to the television, and Mulder couldn't blame him.

On-screen, the scout leader dragged a hand over his face. "I never should've gotten close to their ship."

"Whose ship?" one of the air force investigators asked.

Mulder knew what was coming.

After a dramatic pause, the scout leader finally spoke. "Aliens."

The Major said the word along with him.

"I bet he burned himself while he was building a campfire," Gimble said. "And he didn't want to lose his job."

"Being a scout leader isn't really a job," Mulder pointed out. "They don't get paid."

"Gary is a skeptic." The Major rose from his chair and turned off the VHS player. "He doesn't know the truth."

"I'm not a skeptic." Gimble leaned forward and dropped his head in his hands, exasperated. "Do you think President Carter would let anyone put a show like that on the air if aliens really existed?"

The Major looked at his son. "By telling everyone that aliens and UFOs exist, the government is proving they don't."

Mulder nodded. The argument made a certain kind of sense. People expected the government to keep secrets. "Your dad has a point."

"You don't actually believe any of this alien stuff, do you?" Gimble gave Mulder an incredulous look.

"Anything is possible. It wouldn't be the first time that the government lied. Look what happened with Watergate." Mulder remembered hearing about the Watergate scandal on the news. It felt like the moment in *The Wizard of Oz* when Dorothy pulled back the curtain on the wizard.

He had witnessed firsthand how easily people accepted the explanations they were given. After his sister vanished, the authorities had conducted a massive search. When it turned up nothing, they decided Samantha's disappearance was an isolated incident— and overnight, everyone on the island did, too.

Except Mulder.

"Watergate will look like a bunch of children arguing on the playground compared to what our so-called government is involved in this time. They think they're in control, but they aren't the architects behind the design," the Major said.

Gimble blew out a loud breath and slumped against the sofa, tossing one of his game dice in the air. He seemed to have heard this before.

The Major rushed over to the map. "The world is in chaos. War, famine." He tapped an article on the map. "And crime. But Chaos can't exist without Law."

Chaos can't exist without order, was probably what the Major meant, but Mulder wasn't about to correct him. "Mind if I take a look?"

The Major stood taller. "Go ahead."

Mulder moved closer to the gigantic map of the Washington, DC, metro area taped to the wall. Colored pushpins marked specific locations, and the Major had strung a web of lines between them—the waterfront in Southwest DC; a residential area in Annapolis, Maryland; a stretch of forest in Severn, Maryland.

Newspaper articles with grainy pictures were pinned next to each location, along with random items, like half-finished word searches, glossy black-and-white crime scene photos that looked real, and fortunes from fortune cookies. A mug shot of a woman with mascara smeared down her face, after she was charged with pimping teenage girls, was pinned next to a *Washington Post* headline about a madam whose body was found in a waterfront dumpster. Under the Annapolis pushpin, the Major had saved a longer article with the headline FATAL OVERDOSE EXPOSES ANNAPOLIS DOCTOR'S REAL PROFESSION. He had circled the phrase *opiate-dealing psychiatrist discovered dead*. Mulder's gaze followed the black line from the Annapolis pin to the Severn pin, where the Major had taped a newspaper clipping about a man who had been killed in the woods by wild animals.

"What is all this?" Mulder asked without taking his eyes off the map.

"You don't want to hear about it," Gimble said from his spot on the sofa.

"Actually, I do."

The Major glanced around the room before he answered. "I'm tracking murders in the metro area."

"But it says the psychiatrist overdosed."

"Do you believe everything you read, Mulder?" the Major asked.

Mulder smiled, thinking about his American history test. "No, sir."

"There's only one book you need." The Major sorted through a stack of books under the map and slid a thin green paperback from the middle.

"Tell me when it's over," Gimble called out.

The Major handed the book to Mulder. On the cover a warrior with snow-white hair and skin held a black sword above his head below the title—*Stormbringer*. It was the same book he'd seen multiple copies of earlier.

The one the Major had started reading after Gimble's mom died.

"Michael Moorcock figured out what was happening before the rest of us," the Major said, tapping on the author's name. "He realized mankind had upset the balance between Chaos and Law, throwing the world into chaos."

Mulder wasn't sure what a fantasy novel had to do with it, but the Major was right about one thing. The world was out of control. People were killing one another in wars, and on the streets, with drugs and violence.

"It's an interesting theory." Mulder handed the novel back to the Major and watched as Gimble's dad slid it back into the stack.

"I have proof," the Major continued. "I discovered a pattern. They were not random murders and accidents, like the press reported." He gestured at the map. "All these people were murdered, and their deaths are connected."

"How do you figure? The guy in Severn got attacked by wild animals." Mulder moved closer to the map. Maybe he had missed something. "How are their deaths connected? Did the victims know each other?" He felt guilty for encouraging the Major's delusions, but he wanted to hear his theory.

"No. But they did have one important thing in common."

"Dad!" Gimble bolted off the sofa. It was the first time Mulder had ever heard Gimble refer to his father as anything other than the Major. "Mulder doesn't need to hear your theory. We talked about this."

"Your friend wants to know the truth, Gary. He doesn't want to live in the dark like *you* do."

Mulder felt the tension ratchet up in the room. It reminded him of the heated interactions he had with his own father. He didn't want to put Gimble in that position, but if he didn't hear the Major out now, it might cause more drama.

"It's okay." Mulder gave Gimble a bored look, as if he were throwing the old guy a bone.

Gimble nodded, giving him the go-ahead.

"What did the victims have in common?" Mulder asked.

After a long, uncomfortable silence, the Major cleared his throat. "They were all abducted by aliens."

Mulder almost laughed, but the look on the Major's face made it clear that he was serious.

"The clues are here if you know what to look for," the Major added. "I'll show you."

"He has to get home," Gimble said, signaling Mulder.

"Yeah. My dad is probably back from work by now."

"What about the telescope?" the Major asked.

"I'll check it out next time."

"We'll talk more then." The Major turned suddenly and ducked into the kitchen.

"I'm sorry," Gimble whispered. "I should've known he would go all *Close Encounters* on you. You'd better get out of here before he comes back and tells you his theory about why Abraham Lincoln was really assassinated."

Mulder was halfway to the door when the Major returned, carrying a cereal box.

"Wait." He reached into the box and tossed a few handfuls of sugar-coated cornflakes on the floor. "I have something for you."

"That's okay, sir. I had a big lunch."

For a moment, the Major seemed confused, but he shook it off. He reached into the box again and pulled out a book—a green paperback exactly like the one he had pulled out earlier. "Take this." He offered it to Mulder.

"I wouldn't want to take one of your books."

"Just take it," Gimble said in a low voice, heading for the front door. "He probably has fifty or sixty copies in the house."

The Major shoved the book into Mulder's hand. "There are no coincidences. You and Gary meeting, and him bringing you here today, it was all part of a bigger plan. *Stormbringer* has answers. Moorcock understood *their* ways."

Mulder knew he was referring to aliens again. He held up the copy of *Stormbringer* as Gimble pushed him toward the door. "Thanks, sir. I'll read it."

"Or burn it," Gimble muttered under his breath as Mulder slipped outside.

"Keep your eyes open, Fox Mulder," the Major called after him.

Before Gimble shut the door, Mulder heard the Major say one last thing. "The truth is out there."

CHAPTER 4

Mulder Residence
6:18 P.M.

Mulder was used to ideas getting stuck in his head. Usually, they came from *Star Trek* episodes or books on quantum physics. A retired military conspiracy theorist was a first. But as Mulder walked back to the school parking lot to pick up his car, he couldn't stop thinking about his conversation with the Major—and it was still on his mind as he drove to his dad's apartment.

After listening to Gimble's dad talk about aliens and running an imaginary black ops unit, it seemed crazy to take him seriously, but the Major had said something that made perfect sense to Mulder because he believed it, too.

There are no coincidences.

When Samantha disappeared, people on the island had called it a coincidence. As if a kidnapper just went out for a stroll that night and happened to pass Mulder's house when he was suddenly struck by an overwhelming urge to abduct a kid?

Yeah, right.

What were the odds?

He was still thinking about it when he walked into the apartment. The television was on. For once, his father was home before him.

"Dad?" Mulder dropped his backpack in the hallway and grabbed a handful of sunflower seeds from a bag on the kitchen counter. He used to hate them and the shells his father left all over the house, and they still reminded him of birdseed. But two years ago he had started craving them out of the blue, and he'd been eating them ever since. At least they kind of made it feel like home.

"In here," his dad called from the master bedroom.

Mulder's dad had rented the apartment when his parents separated, which was code for getting divorced. The place was nice, but it felt more like a hotel than a home. Everything in the second-floor walk-up was brand-new—from the cassette tape player that his dad never used and the expensive toaster that never worked, to the desk in Mulder's room that was the identical twin to the one in his room back in Chilmark (minus the *Dune* quotes written all over it).

Living with his dad for the school year—the "getting-to-know-each-other-better experiment," as Mulder called it—wasn't much different from the pre-separation status quo of ignoring each other.

When Mulder reached his dad's room and spotted the open suitcase at the end of the bed, it reminded him of the other reason the apartment felt like a hotel. His dad was always leaving on a business trip or returning from one.

"Going somewhere?" Mulder leaned against the door frame, looking bored. If his dad didn't care enough to spend any time with him, Mulder wasn't going to let it bother him.

"New Mexico. It's a quick trip. I'll be back on Monday." His dad didn't look up from the shirts he was folding. "I want you to head over to Georgetown tomorrow. Spend some time on campus like we talked about. The sooner you make a decision, the better."

Meaning the sooner Mulder made the decision his dad wanted him make. "Acceptance letters don't come for two more weeks." Unless, of course, your dad used his connections at the State Department to make sure that you were already accepted to the college he wanted you to attend. "I still have time to decide."

His father tossed the shirt in his hand on the bed. "There's nothing to decide. Kids don't turn down acceptances to Georgetown University."

Mulder crossed his arms. "Of course they do, or there wouldn't be a waiting list. And I thought you were coming with me to show me 'the lay of the land.' What happened to playing tour guide?" His dad had never attended Georgetown, unless the campus tour counted, but he had the prospective students brochure memorized.

"I'm going out of town, remember?" He gestured at the suitcase, irritated.

"Does everyone at the State Department work weekends, or just you?" Mulder sounded more bitter than usual.

"Most people don't have my level of responsibility, and the project I'm working on is entering an important phase." His father arranged the shirts neatly in the suitcase.

"I bet."

"I tried to get out of going, if that makes you feel any better." His dad almost sounded sincere. "I know you don't understand, but what I do is important. It's bigger than me. I'm trying to do some good in the world. . . ." He stared at his half-packed suitcase, and for a second, he looked miserable.

Mulder almost felt sorry for his dad, but it didn't last. Whatever prompted this heartfelt share session couldn't make up for the past few years. Work was always his father's priority, even when his family was falling apart, which didn't make any sense to Mulder. As far as he was concerned, nothing would ever be as important as his sister and finding out what had happened to her.

His dad looked up and shook off any genuine emotion he might have been feeling. "It's not like I planned to be out of town.

I'm not thrilled about the idea of Phoebe staying here while I'm away."

Phoebe was arriving late Sunday night. They had planned the trip months ago, after he realized they had spring break at the same time.

"Why? You don't trust me?" Mulder clenched his jaw. Based on this conversation, the answer was obvious.

His father scoffed, "Give me a break. You're a seventeen-year-old with a stack of *Playboy* magazines stashed under your bed."

"I'll be eighteen in October. Or did you forget *again*?" Mulder shot back. Last year his dad had called him a day late to wish him happy birthday. "I can write it down if that will make it easier to remember."

Instead of apologizing for being a crappy parent, Bill Mulder pulled out the big guns. "Maybe I should call Phoebe's parents and tell them she can't come?" He reached for the phone on the nightstand.

As much as Mulder wanted to call his father's bluff, he knew his dad would go through with it. And knowing Phoebe, her parents probably didn't know much about the trip. So, for once, Mulder kept his mouth shut. He couldn't screw up his chance to see Phoebe. He missed the hell out of her.

"No smart comment?" his dad asked, reveling in the lame victory.

There's the Bill Mulder I know. Cold, distant, and condescending.

"Just let her come." Mulder forced out the words through gritted teeth. "Please."

"Sleep on the sofa and don't make me regret trusting you."

"No problem." Mulder almost laughed. His dad didn't even know basic things about him—like the fact that he already spent every night on the sofa.

Mulder retreated to the living room, turned on the TV set, and slumped on a stiff leather armchair. A little background noise would drown out his dad's annoying voice if he ended up on one of his secret phone calls that Mulder didn't give a crap about.

Two more months until graduation, and I'm outta here.

Then he could go back to living with his mom until August, when he left for college. If he figured out where he was going by then.

A newscaster's voice droned on in the background. Mulder wasn't really listening until he heard the words *missing girl*. He jerked forward and sat on the edge of the chair, listening.

"Sarah Lowe vanished from her home just before nine o'clock last night," the reporter said as a photo popped up in the corner of the screen. A little girl with big brown eyes and crooked dirty-blond pigtails, wearing zip-up pajamas with elephants on them, smiled back at him. She looked around the same age as Samantha when she disappeared.

Mulder's skin went cold.

The newscast switched to another feed. A woman with puffy eyes and the same shade of dirty-blond hair as Sarah stood at a podium between her husband and the DC police chief, clutching a wad of tissues.

"Sarah was playing in the living room, and the power went out," Mrs. Lowe said between ragged sobs. "So I went down to the basement to check the breaker. I would've taken Sarah with me, but she hates it down there. She gets scared. She was only alone for two minutes." Her breath hitched and she dissolved into tears again. Sarah's dad put his arm around his wife's shoulders and tried to console her.

Mulder remembered his mother had the same desperate look right after Samantha was taken.

The police chief turned to Sarah's mom. "If this is too difficult—"

"I can do it," Mrs. Lowe said, and looked straight into the camera. "When I came back, Sarah was gone and the front door was wide open."

Mulder's stomach lurched and he almost puked.

The power went out and the front door was open. Just like when Samantha was taken. The details were so similar.

Sarah's photo appeared on the TV screen again, and the police chief took over. "Sarah Lowe has blond hair and brown eyes, and a small scar above her right eyebrow."

Mulder focused on the photo: Sarah's happy-kid grin, minus

a front tooth. The dimple in her left cheek. Gray elephants marching across her white pajamas, except for the brown one above the top of the zipper. Mulder leaned closer and realized it wasn't an elephant at all. It was a brown stain, shaped sort of like a hippo.

"The search is ongoing. If anyone has information related to Sarah Lowe's disappearance, please call the tip line."

Mulder stood in front of the TV set in a daze. He didn't even remember getting up from the chair. All he could think about was Samantha and Sarah Lowe, gray elephants and a brown hippo-shaped spot—and two front doors—both hanging wide open. He was still standing there when his dad walked into the living room and turned off the television.

"Didn't you hear me calling you?" His father's harsh tone yanked Mulder back to reality.

Did you hear about the missing little girl? That was what Mulder wanted to ask, but he settled on "Obviously not."

If he brought up the newscast, his dad would inevitably make a rude comment about Mulder's "unhealthy obsession" with Samantha's disappearance, causing Mulder to fire back with a rude comment of his own. Phoebe's visit would be over before it started. And he *had* to talk to her about this.

"I don't appreciate your attitude, Mulder." His father stalked down the hallway to his room. "One day that smart mouth of yours is going to get you in real trouble."

The bedroom door slammed, and it took Mulder a minute to fully absorb the significance of what had just happened. In the last hour, his father had managed to ruin his night, proving, yet again, that Mulder couldn't count on him. But something else happened, too.

Mulder smiled.

He had finally gotten his dad to stop calling him Fox.

After the eleven o'clock news, Mulder's eyes started feeling heavy, not that it mattered. Insomnia won its nightly battle 90 percent of the time. Sleep equaled nightmares: the chance to relive the worst night of his life over and over.

Mulder's mind flashed on Sarah Lowe's photo from the news. Another flash hit, and he found himself staring at the face of a different eight-year-old girl. . . .

Samantha sitting cross-legged on the living room floor of the Chilmark house with a Stratego game board in front of her.

The news was on in the background—a report about Watergate. Fox's favorite show was coming on in a few minutes, and he couldn't miss it. He captured one of his sister's Stratego game pieces and took it off the board.

"Do we have to watch this, Fox?" she whined.

"Leave it. I'm watching The Magician at nine."

"Mom and Dad said I could watch a movie," she argued.

"They're next door at the Galbrands'. And they said I'm in charge." As far as he was concerned, that meant he was in charge of the TV, too.

Samantha got up and changed the channel to a stupid Western.

"Hey! Get out of my life!" Fox yelled.

Samantha shrieked in his ear, but she wasn't getting her way tonight.

He switched it back and stood up, towering over her. "I'm watching The Magician."

The lights went out suddenly, and that was where the memory got fuzzy. He remembered his heart pounding and hearing Samantha scream his name. "Fox!"

Then the room faded. . . .

When Fox regained consciousness minutes later, he was lying on his back in the living room, staring at the cracks in the ceiling.

Why was he sleeping on the floor out there, instead of in his bedroom? What time was it? He remembered arguing with Samantha and the power going out.

Something was wrong.

Fox bolted upright, an overwhelming sense of dread clutching at his chest. His gaze shot to the rug where his sister had been sitting a few minutes ago. Stratego pieces lay scattered across the board, but no Samantha.

Where did she go?

"Samantha?" Fox called out. No response. Instead he heard a familiar creaking sound behind him, and he turned around slowly.

The front door of the house was wide open.

Fox ran to the door, heart pounding. The sidewalks in his quiet neighborhood were dark, except where the lampposts cast pale halos on the sidewalks. Had Samantha gone outside? Maybe she was next door with their parents?

But as he raced down the front steps and into the middle of the street, Fox knew the truth.

His sister was gone.

CHAPTER 5

Mulder woke up earlier than usual the next morning. Avoiding his father was an art, and he didn't want to be home when his dad left for the airport. The nightmare about Samantha already had him on edge.

He jogged the same route every Saturday—down New Hampshire Avenue, past the convenience store, around Rock Creek Cemetery, and back to the apartment. Running cleared his head, and if he lucked out, he would pass a hot girl. Not that any of them compared to Phoebe.

Today, even Phoebe's long legs and killer smile couldn't take his mind off the missing kids. First the little boy, Billy Christian, and now Sarah Lowe. What were the odds of two children in the metro area disappearing within a week and a half of each other? What if the police didn't find them?

Did Billy and Sarah have any brothers or sisters? Were their siblings blaming themselves for what happened? He wouldn't wish that kind of misery on anyone.

Except for the bastard who took Samantha.

He pushed away the thought and focused on the statues coming into view.

Rock Creek Cemetery was an older cemetery, dominated by mausoleums with stone archangels standing sentinel on the rooftops. His favorite crypt had four statues, located on the corners of the slab roof. Each angel held a sword, as if they were guarding the souls of the people inside.

Mulder jogged up the hill and rounded the bend, debating whether to take a break and check out the warrior angels, when he noticed the police cars. He stopped and took in the scene below. A row of mausoleums was sectioned off with yellow crime scene tape, and a white coroner's van was parked inside the perimeter.

Behind the tape, uniformed officers were talking to a groundskeeper and a well-dressed man consulting a map and a bound ledger. Nearby, two detectives stood in front of an older brick mausoleum speaking with a middle-aged woman wearing funeral attire. The woman glanced at the mausoleum, inching farther and farther away from it, but her high heels kept getting stuck in the grass.

One of the detectives was tall and thin, with squinty eyes, and the button-down under his suit jacket was wrinkled as if he'd slept in it. The other detective was short, and his gut hung over the waistband of his slacks. His face glistened with sweat beneath a black fedora. They reminded Mulder of Laurel and Hardy.

Police squad cars and a news van had parked across from the taped-off area. Two cameramen toting boxy video cameras were trying to talk their way past a cop, who seemed to be in charge of keeping them away from the crime scene. Behind the officer, a group of people dressed in black huddled together just outside the yellow tape, not far from reporters vying for prime spots.

Something serious must have happened to attract this much attention. Mulder could hear Phoebe's voice in his head, saying, *Whatever's going on is none of your business, Fox.*

But other people were hanging around. Did it really matter if he stayed to check things out? Wondering what happened would drive him crazy, and for an insomniac, that guaranteed another sleepless night.

Phoebe always says I should get more sleep, he thought, mentally preparing his defense.

Mulder followed the footpath around to the side of the taped perimeter, then walked down the hill. As he moved closer, a reporter called out to the detectives, "What's going on over there? Give us something."

A uniformed officer approached the tape, waving his hand at

them as if he were scattering gnats. "Nobody's talking to you, so have some decency and get outta here. The family's been through enough this morning."

Mulder noticed a guy around his age leaning against a tree, looking bored. He was wearing a black suit, with an untucked gray button-down shirt, as if he was dressed for a funeral like the other people in the group near the crime scene tape. Maybe he knew something?

Mulder walked over and stood next to the tree. "I wonder what happened."

The guy sighed. "We showed up to say some prayers while they put my grandmother's casket in the crypt, and a little kid was already in her spot." His eyes darted to a huge weeping angel on top of another mausoleum. "I'll probably be stuck here all day now. I hate cemeteries. They give me the creeps."

"Was it a mix-up?" Mulder already knew the answer. Interring someone in the wrong crypt wouldn't warrant detectives and a coroner.

"Nah. The cops are saying the kid was murdered." He rubbed the back of his neck. "I didn't see the body, but my mom and the dudes from the cemetery did, and they flipped out."

"That still sucks. Sorry about your grandmother."

The guy shrugged. "Don't be. She was mean as hell. She used to spank us with a plastic hairbrush. I just feel bad for the kid they found."

"Me too." Mulder nodded at the guy and walked over by the crime scene. He inched toward the trees between the taped-off area and the next mausoleum.

A bald man wearing a jacket with CORONER on the back signaled to a uniformed police officer. "Let the detectives know that we're bringing out the body. And get the family out of here."

"Sure thing." The cop followed the instructions, and Laurel and Hardy trudged over to the coroner.

The detectives lowered their voices, and Mulder only caught snippets of their conversation. "What kind of sick—?"

"I've never seen anything like—"

"—the kind of thing that keeps you up at night."

Something had them rattled. What was so disturbing?

"Can you tell us what happened?" someone called out.

The police officer was holding up the crime scene tape for the family, and the reporters had descended on the woman wearing the black dress and heels.

"What did you see?"

"I heard an officer say there's a child in there."

"Can you confirm that information?"

"Back off." The cop threw his arm up between the woman and the reporters who were grilling her. "I said, back up *now*, or I'll arrest you."

It took another cop to clear a path for her and the rest of the family.

The coroner's van was parked with the back facing the row of mausoleums, which ranged in size from a storage shed to a garage. The spaces between them offered the perfect hiding place. He could easily slip into one of the gaps and eavesdrop while they loaded the gurney back into the van.

Mulder looked around. The guy in the black suit had taken off with his family, and half the reporters had followed them, while the other half were still giving Laurel and Hardy the third degree. Everyone was preoccupied.

It's now or never.

He slid into one of the narrow spaces and waited for what felt like an hour, though it was probably closer to ten minutes.

The coroner finally knocked on the door of the van and his team got out to unload a gurney from the back of the vehicle and follow the coroner into the small mausoleum. The crypt wasn't gigantic, like the one with the warrior angel statues on the roof. The brick structure was probably designed to hold two people or three people, tops. They managed to get most of the gurney inside, but the bottom third stuck out.

The reporters rushed toward the van. Between the crime scene tape and the strategic parking job, they couldn't see anything. But Mulder had the perfect view. A black body bag was strapped to the gurney, the ends sagging because the body inside was too small to fill it.

A female detective with her badge hooked on the waistband of her jeans ducked under the tape and approached the coroner. "I'm Detective Perez with the Special Operations Division. Mind if I take a look?" she asked.

"Do you have kids?" the coroner asked. "If you do, you might not want to see this."

She pointed at the bag with the phantom of a child's shape inside. "Not every woman has kids. Open it."

Mulder scooted forward until he was standing at the mouth of the narrow space. The coroner walked around to the other side of the gurney, shielding the top of the bag with his body. Detective Perez moved closer, blocking Mulder's line of sight.

The coroner leaned over the body bag and unzipped it halfway.

Detective Perez cursed under her breath and lowered her voice. "Is that Billy Christian? The boy who disappeared nine days ago? Is that a bird on his chest?"

A bird?

"Yes to both questions," the coroner confirmed. "But I can't go on record without a formal ID."

Mulder pressed himself against the stone, attempting to get a better angle.

"I've seen lots of twisted crap, but nothing like this," Detective Perez said. The slight change in her stance allowed Mulder to catch a glimpse over her shoulder.

A little boy lay in the bag. His skin had a gray cast that was unnatural and terrifying. In movies, dead people looked like they were sleeping, with a little fake blood splattered around for effect. This kid did *not* look asleep. The ashen color of his skin and the stillness of his body gave Mulder goose bumps.

"You think we're dealing with a satanic cult?" The coroner sounded concerned.

"Most likely," Detective Perez said. "But it's hard to know until we figure out if this bird, and whatever they did to it, means anything."

A black-and-white bird, no bigger than a soda can, rested on the boy's chest, as dead as the child.

Something was sticking out of the bird's body.

When Mulder realized what he was looking at, he pressed his mouth against the inside of his elbow to keep from heaving. Arrows protruded from the bird's body—fanning out around it, the way little kids draw the rays of the sun.

Two.

Four.

Six.

Eight. Or was it nine? Mulder counted the points again. *Eight.* But the bird wasn't the worst part, not by a long shot.

The little boy was dressed in white pajamas, with gray elephants marching across his fleece-covered arms and chest. Gray-and-white elephant pajamas—exactly like the ones Sarah Lowe had been wearing when she was kidnapped.

Mulder swallowed, his heart galloping in his chest. The team who brought over the gurney lifted the boy slightly and tilted him in Mulder's direction. As they raised the body withered white flower petals fluttered to the ground. His eyes went straight to the top of the zipper on the child's pajamas.

Gray elephants. And one brown hippo.

The stain was there, in the exact same spot where Mulder had seen it on Sarah Lowe's pajamas, on the newscast.

Shouting erupted behind the coroner. The reporters and the cops were at it again.

"Zip it up," Detective Perez said. "We can't afford to let the press see the body." She stood up straight, obscuring Mulder's view again.

He heard the zipper close, but his heartbeat didn't return to normal. If anything, it pounded faster. The little boy was wearing the missing girl's pajamas, which meant that whoever killed the boy and left him in an old lady's crypt, holding a dead bird, was the same person who had taken Sarah Lowe.

He sidestepped toward the back of the gap between the mausoleums and came out at the other end, behind them. Bile rose in his throat. He couldn't get the photo of Sarah Lowe's dimpled smile and her elephant pajamas out of his head. Or the image of Billy Christian in a plastic body bag, wearing those same pajamas.

Mulder bolted through the grass, dodging avenging angels carved from stone and trees with thin limbs that reminded him of arrows. He didn't need anyone to confirm that both children had been kidnapped by the same person. Mulder *knew* it. His memory recorded details the way a camera captured an image—with precision and accuracy—exactly as they appeared in that moment.

One thought replayed over and over as he ran.

There are no coincidences.

CHAPTER 6

Mulder returned to the apartment out of breath. At least his dad was gone. He still couldn't wrap his head around what he'd seen at the cemetery. Someone had abducted two kids, and the way Sarah Lowe had been taken also mirrored Samantha's kidnapping—the time of night, Sarah sitting in the living room, the power going out just before she was taken, and the front door left open afterward.

Did the same person take Samantha?

The possibility got under his skin. Actually, crawling around underneath it was closer to the truth. His nerve endings buzzed and he couldn't stop moving. As he paced back and forth across the living room, the thought burrowed deeper and deeper with every step.

There was only one way to figure out if Sarah Lowe and Billy Christian's kidnappings were connected to Samantha's disappearance. Mulder needed to find more information about Billy Christian and the details related to his abduction.

Because I've been down this road before.

After Samantha disappeared, he became obsessed with the idea that whoever had taken Samantha could've been the same person who abducted a girl named Wendy Kelly, in New Haven, Connecticut, the day before. Wendy was kidnapped from her house, just like Samantha. But every time Mulder brought it up, his father bit his head off, and the small-time island cops refused to investigate.

The kitchen phone rang and Mulder jumped. He let it ring seven times before he finally answered it. "Hello?"

"Fox? Is that you, sweetheart? It's Mom."

As much as he loved his mother, he wasn't in the mood to talk to anyone. "Yeah. Hi, Mom. How's everything going?"

"Fine, but the house feels so much bigger now that I'm here alone."

"I could come back," he offered. Moving in with his dad for senior year had been her idea in the first place, not his. He had gone along with it to make her happy, with the smallest shred of hope that his father might change.

"Don't be ridiculous, honey," she said. "You're graduating in two months. I'm fine. Really. With your father gone, the house feels peaceful. Of course, I would love it if you were here, too. I'm not sure Phoebe would survive until summer if she weren't going to visit you. I ran into her at the library last week, and she spent fifteen minutes explaining why the technology in *Star Wars* could be developed within your lifetimes."

"That sounds like Phoebe." His best friend was the only person smart enough to challenge him, an activity she considered a hobby. It was one of the reasons he harbored a not-so-secret crush on her.

"I should've invited her to come over and take a look at the vacuum cleaner for me." She paused, and he heard her banging something around. "Because the stupid ElectroVac your father insisted on buying from that salesman is broken *again*."

"I'll fix it as soon as I get home."

She sighed. "Thank you. But I can't wait until June to vacuum the floors. Enough about appliances. Are you and your father getting along?"

If ignoring each other qualifies as getting along, Mulder thought, before he gave his mom the response she wanted to hear. "As well as we usually do."

A timer buzzed in the background on the other end of the line.

"I have to take a casserole out of the oven. Do you want to hold on for a minute?"

"That's okay. We can talk later." He wanted to see if there were any news reports on TV about Billy Christian.

"All right. I love you," she said.

"Me too."

It was just after eleven o'clock when Mulder hung up the phone, and the news didn't air again until noon. But finding a dead child was big news. Maybe the local stations would interrupt game shows and sitcoms to report real news. He paced until noon, changing the channel every few minutes to make sure he didn't miss any coverage. But they never broke in with a special report. When the news finally came on, he was going stir-crazy.

On TV, a reporter stood in front of the yellow crime scene tape Mulder had seen that morning. Her silky purple blouse had a huge bow in the front that looked as if it might strangle her any minute. "I'm here at Rock Creek Cemetery in Washington, DC, where a child's body was discovered in a mausoleum early this morning. The child has been identified as eight-year-old Billy Christian, the boy who disappeared from his home nine days ago. The discovery is a shocking blow to the community, especially in the wake of Sarah Lowe's disappearance two nights ago."

The detective with the big gut ducked under the tape, attracting the reporter's attention. She rushed over and shoved a big microphone in his face. "Detective? Has the police department uncovered any clues to the murder of Billy Christian? Is this case related to Sarah Lowe's kidnapping?"

"The two cases are unrelated." The detective shot the reporter a warning glance, but she was already done with him and facing the camera again.

"I'll remain at the scene to bring you updates on the investigation as they develop," she assured her viewers. "Now Brian North has more on this story."

The coverage cut to another reporter with a bad comb-over. He was speaking with the groundskeeper Mulder had seen near the mausoleum that morning. "I'm here with Howard Redding, grounds supervisor at Rock Creek Cemetery. Mr. Redding, I was told that you discovered Billy Christian's body. Walk us through what you saw."

The groundskeeper cleared his throat. "I unlocked the door of the crypt to make sure everything was in order for the interment. That's when I saw the boy's body, laid out on a bed of flower petals, like a saint. Except all the flowers were dead." He rubbed the back of his neck and shook his head. "And he had a dead bird lying on his chest, like the whole thing was part of a satanic ritual."

"Turn off that camera!" A cop rushed into the frame and ushered the groundskeeper away.

The reporter turned his questions on the cop. "Officer, this sounds like a ritualistic killing. Are we dealing with a cult? Should residents be concerned?"

The cop's jaw twitched and his eyes darted to the camera. "Nobody said anything about a cult. We're done here." He moved off camera, and the lens zoomed in on the reporter.

"If the police have any new information, they're keeping it under wraps for now. But WJLA News will continue to report on any developments in the case."

Mulder had spent five years waiting for developments in his sister's case, and waiting for answers he might never get.

In that moment, he made himself a promise.

This time he wouldn't fail.

He would find this little girl before it was too late.

CHAPTER 7

"What took you so long?" Mulder asked when Gimble finally arrived at the apartment. "I called forty-five minutes ago." And he'd spent every minute since then changing the channel, searching for more news, and wearing a hole in the carpet.

"You're lucky I still had the phone in my room. The Major usually confiscates it right away to check for alien transmitters." Gimble pushed past him, with his hands shoved in the pockets of his blue velour warm-up jacket. "And to answer your original question, I had to take the bus. I don't have a car. And you could've offered to pick me up, since *you* do."

Mulder changed the channel again. The same commercial was still playing. "I can't leave. I'm waiting for the six o'clock news to start." He hadn't filled Gimble in on the details when he called.

"Since when are you interested in the news?" Gimble asked. "Is NASA holding a press conference or something? Because that's not an actual emergency. And you said this was an emergency."

Mulder changed the channel one more time.

Nothing.

Gimble pointed at the TV. "And why do you keep doing that?"

No news about Billy Christian or Sarah Lowe. He refused to think about the possibility that she might be dead, too. He kicked a cardboard box full of crap his dad still hadn't unpacked.

Then he hit Gimble with the story. "Does a dead kid holding a bird with arrows sticking out of it count as an emergency?"

"Back up." Gimble flopped down on the sofa behind him. "You mean the kid from the cemetery?"

Mulder took a deep breath. "Yeah."

"I know all about it. The Major was sitting in front of the TV set with a legal pad, taking notes all morning. A news reporter interviewed a man who said something about a dead bird and cults, but they didn't mention arrows." Gimble flicked his hair out of his eyes and leaned forward, watching Mulder. "How do you know there were arrows sticking out of . . . Did you say they were in the *kid*?"

Mulder clutched at his hair, frustrated. "The *bird*. They were sticking out of the bird."

"Hit rewind and start at the beginning," Gimble said.

"I was jogging past Rock Creek Cemetery this morning, and I saw the body. They were bringing it out of the mausoleum in a body bag, and a detective unzipped it." Mulder paced. "The kid was lying on top of dead rose petals, and there was a black-and-white bird on his chest with arrows stuck in its body."

Gimble's eyes went wide. "No way."

Mulder switched the channel again.

"It's on," Gimble said, jumping to his feet.

A newscaster stood on the sidewalk in front of a police station. "I'm here at the Third District Precinct, in Southwest Washington, DC, where officers are sifting through clues in the case involving the body of an eight-year-old boy that was discovered this morning at Rock Creek Cemetery."

The reporter noticed a detective with a badge clipped to his belt leaving the precinct, and he rushed over with the microphone. "Detective? Have the police uncovered any clues related to the murder of Billy Christian? According to our sources, the carcass of a bird was found with the body, in what appeared to be a ritualistic killing. Are we dealing with a cult?"

"I don't care what your *sources* told you. If you cared about that kid, you'd get out of here and let us do our jobs. The chief already made a statement." The cop looked straight into the camera. "I've got nothing else to say."

The detective stormed out of the frame, and the camera shifted back to the reporter. "If the metropolitan police department has made any progress in the case, they aren't sharing it with the public."

The network logo appeared on the screen, followed by a commercial for dishwashing liquid. Mulder stared at the television, stunned.

"He didn't say anything about the pajamas," he said to himself.

"What pajamas?" Gimble asked.

"We need to call Phoebe." Mulder wandered to the kitchen.

At the mention of a girl's name, Gimble scrambled after him. "Who's Phoebe?"

Mulder reached for the black rotary phone on the wall. "My best friend back home."

"Your best friend is a *girl*? And you never mentioned her before? Is she pretty?" Gimble's questions barely registered with Mulder.

"She'll help," he said, hoping the person he trusted most in the world could tell him what to do next. Or talk him out of what he was already thinking about doing.

"I should get on the phone in the other room. Since I'm your right-hand man on this," Gimble suggested. When Mulder didn't argue, his friend bolted out of the kitchen.

Mulder dialed Phoebe's number, and the line crackled when Gimble picked up the other extension. "Hello?"

"It's still ringing."

Under normal circumstances, Mulder wouldn't have let

Gimble join the call, but he was *in his head*, as Phoebe called it—his thoughts focused on one thing.

"Hello?" Phoebe picked up on the fourth ring. Her voice usually calmed Mulder, but tonight it only made him anxious to see her.

"I need your help," he blurted out.

"What's wrong?" Her tone switched to all business.

"Someone is abducting kids in the DC area. A boy turned up dead, and a little girl is still missing." Mulder was talking too fast, but he had to get it all out. "The girl is eight years old, Phoebe."

There was silence on the other end of the line.

"I know what you're going to say . . . ," Mulder barreled ahead.

"Don't get involved, Fox."

"But I'm already involved. I saw the boy's body—"

"You *what?*" Phoebe flipped out. "Do I even want to know how you managed that?"

"He was jogging by the cemetery when they found the kid," Gimble said, ignoring the fact that Mulder hadn't introduced him or mentioned he was on the line. "It's not like he broke into the morgue or anything weird."

"What a relief." Phoebe laid on the sarcasm. "And who are you?"

"Oh, yeah. Sorry." Gimble cleared his throat. "This is Gimble, Mulder's best friend."

She snorted. "Let's get one thing straight. I'm Fox's best friend."

"How come she gets to call you Fox?"

"Gimble!" Mulder snapped.

"Are you the guy who plays D and D?" Phoebe asked.

"That's me." Gimble could barely contain his excitement. "So Mulder told you about me? Did he tell you that I have sixteen experience points?"

"Gimble!" Mulder yelled.

"Sorry," Gimble mumbled. "Tell her about the dead bird."

"Dead birds?" Phoebe's tone switched from *What have you gotten yourself into this time?* to *What the hell is going on and how do I stop it?*

"Bird," Gimble said. "There was only one."

"Gimble!" Phoebe and Mulder shouted at the same time.

"I'll be quiet now."

Mulder took a deep breath. "It's a long story, and I swear I'll fill you in on every detail. But right now I need your advice."

"Whatever it is, *don't* do it," Phoebe said immediately.

"Are you going to listen or not?" Once Mulder explained that the kidnappings were connected, he knew she would understand.

"Talk." One word. That was all she gave him.

He had to stay calm or Phoebe would think he was *fixating*, as she called it. "The girl who disappeared was wearing a pair of white zip-up pajamas with gray elephants on them. When they showed her photo on TV, I noticed a brown stain above the top of the zipper. It was shaped like a hippo."

"A hippo?" She was losing her patience. "Is this what you guys do together? Run around and solve mysteries?"

"Umm . . ." Gimble cleared his throat. "I wasn't actually there. So, technically, Mulder was solving it on his own."

"Do you want to hear about the pajamas on the dead body or not?" Mulder asked. Phoebe and Gimble stopped talking, and he picked up where he'd left off. "When they unzipped the body bag at the cemetery, the boy they found was wearing the same pajamas."

Phoebe sighed. "Do you know how many—"

"Not pajamas with the same pattern. I mean the exact same pair of pajamas. The stain was there, right above the zipper."

"It could be a—" she began.

"Don't say 'coincidence,' because we both know you don't believe in them, either."

"She and the Major would get along," Gimble said, working his way back into the conversation.

"Who—?" Phoebe stopped herself. "I'm not going to ask."

Why was she making this so hard? She never doubted him when it came to important things. He tried to stay calm, but panic surged through his veins in fits and bursts, like electricity in a downed telephone wire. "Phoebe, listen to me. You know I only need to see something once to remember it perfectly."

"Words and images, Fox. Not people."

"Not *faces*," Mulder corrected her. "And we're talking about an article of clothing and a stain."

"You can't remember people's faces?" Gimble asked, confused.

Phoebe sighed. "Of course he can, just not any better than the average person. A photographic memory doesn't apply to everything across the board. That's a myth," she explained. "But he's right. He'd never forget the details on someone's clothes."

"Then you believe me?" Relief washed over Mulder.

"It's not a matter of believing you."

He told her the most important part. "Someone dressed the dead boy in the missing girl's pajamas, which means they were kidnapped by the same person. But the police haven't figured it out. They don't realize the cases are connected."

"Let it go, Fox," Phoebe said softly. "It won't bring Samantha back."

"Bring who back?" Gimble realized he was missing something, but Mulder and Phoebe didn't fill him in.

"An eight-year-old girl is missing." Mulder tried to sound normal, like he'd pulled himself together and now he was just stating the facts. Not fixating.

"I know what you're thinking, Fox." Now Phoebe was the one who sounded panicked. "Don't do it."

"Do what?" Gimble asked.

"The police will think you're crazy," she warned.

"But I know something they don't." Mulder's voice rose.

"Just wait until I get there tomorrow night," she pleaded. "I'll help you figure this out. I promise."

He kicked the leg of the kitchen table. "Fine. I won't go."

"I'll see you tomorrow, okay?" Phoebe sounded relieved.

"Okay."

Gimble made it back to the kitchen before Mulder had time to hang up the phone. "I feel like I joined a quest in the middle of the game, and nobody will tell me what's going on."

Mulder headed straight for the front door. He grabbed his car keys off the hook on the way out. "I'll explain in the car."

"You told Phoebe you weren't going wherever the hell you two were talking about." Gimble followed him to his parking spot.

Mulder unlocked the car door. "I lied. I'll apologize tomorrow."

Gimble hopped in fast, clearly worried that his friend might take off without him. Mulder threw the AMC Gremlin into reverse and flipped a U-turn like he was driving a Corvette instead of an orange tin can.

"So where are we going?" Gimble asked.

Dread churned in Mulder's stomach. He didn't want to do this, but he couldn't stop himself. "The police station."

CHAPTER 8

"So who's Samantha?" Gimble asked from where he sat slouched in the passenger seat of Mulder's car.

Mulder's chest tightened, and he almost unleashed on his friend. But how could he when Gimble was riding to the police station with him, even after hearing Phoebe warn Mulder not to go? They had become friends because of their mutual love of *Star Trek* and the TV show *Wonder Woman*, because they both thought Lynda Carter was hot. But Gimble had turned out to be a real friend.

And back then, I didn't even know he had a thing for Farrah, too.

The only person aside from Samantha who had ever trusted Mulder enough to follow him anywhere was Phoebe. Two years ago, when Wendy Kelly was found at a gas station after being missing for three and a half years, Phoebe had ditched school to drive to a hospital in New Haven with him. He had hoped Wendy Kelly could tell him where to find Samantha. Mulder made it all the way to the girl's hospital room door before a doctor intercepted him and kicked him out.

By the time Mulder found a way to get out of the house again and drive to the Kellys' house in New Haven two days later, Wendy and her family were gone. The only thing they left behind was a bag of sunflower seeds spilled on the porch.

If Mulder was dragging Gimble to the police station with him, the least he could do was answer his friend's question.

"Samantha is my younger sister. She disappeared on November 27, almost five and a half years ago. She was eight when it happened." A knot formed at the base of his throat.

And she's out there, somewhere, waiting for me to find her.

Gimble stared at Mulder, stunned. "I don't know what to say. I mean . . . I'm sorry, but that doesn't seem like enough, you know?"

Mulder gave him a small nod.

"When you say she 'disappeared,' what does that mean exactly?"

It was the story Mulder had replayed over and over in his mind—the story he still had nightmares about.

"Forget it," Gimble said quickly. "You probably don't want to talk about it."

He didn't. But whether or not Mulder talked about it, the hollow feeling inside him never went away. "Someone took her."

Gimble fell back against the seat. "And the cops never found her?"

"No."

"Did she wander off or something? Or was it like those film-strips they showed in middle school where creeps offer kids candy and then snatch them?"

Part of Mulder wished it had happened that way. He wished the villain had a face—a police sketch or something to focus on when the rage hit and threatened to consume him. Instead of a sketch, the person responsible stared back at him every morning from the bathroom mirror.

Because I should've saved her.

"Someone kidnapped her from our house," Mulder said before he lost his nerve. "My parents went out, and I was supposed to be watching her. We were in the living room playing Stratego. It was almost nine o'clock, and I was waiting for *The Magician* to start. Samantha wanted to change the channel, and I . . ." He hesitated. "I yelled at her. Then the power went out, and I don't know what happened after that. I must've blacked out. But when I came to, my sister was gone, and our front door was open."

Mulder turned onto 17th Street, and the police precinct came into view. He pulled into the parking lot and turned off the car.

"Thanks for telling me," Gimble said. "I know it's hard. You're the only person I've had over since my mom died and we moved to DC. The Major is a lot to take in."

"He's all right," Mulder offered.

"If by 'all right,' you mean not even remotely normal, then yeah, sure." Gimble looked out the window. "When the cops told us that my mom's car went off the bridge, they said it looked like she did it on purpose. I left that part out before. But I never believed them, and neither did the Major. Losing her broke him. Sometimes I think that's why he became obsessed with that book, *Stormbringer.* My mom loved fantasy novels, and we read them together all the time. She tried to talk my dad into reading *Stormbringer* with her, but he wasn't a big fan of fantasy—which is ironic considering all the crazy stuff he believes in now."

"I get it." Mulder knew it took a lot for Gimble to open up like that and talk about his mom. It made it easier for Mulder to confess his own sins. "I didn't do anything to help my sister that night. So if there's a chance I can help Sarah Lowe, I have to try."

Gimble nodded. "I couldn't help my mom, either. But it's not too late to save that little girl." He opened the car door and got out like a man on a mission, in a Han Solo T-shirt. "Lord Manhammer says, 'A quest is only over if you give up.'"

Mulder and Gimble marched through the glass doors and straight into the action. The precinct didn't have a counter up front separating the entrance from the central room. It was packed with metal desks and file cabinets, mug shots and two-way radios, police officers and criminals.

The precinct wasn't what Mulder had expected. The place felt like the Wild West. Criminals were handcuffed to the desks, yelling and cussing over one another.

"I've never been in a police station before." Gimble eyed a rough-looking guy with a mustache. The guy turned, and Gimble spotted his shoulder holster. "How are we supposed to tell the cops from the criminals?"

The cop noticed Mulder and Gimble and strode toward them. "You boys need some help?"

"I'd like to talk to one of the detectives investigating Sarah Lowe's kidnapping," Mulder said.

The cop raised an eyebrow. "We haven't confirmed that she was kidnapped." It sounded like something official they had to say.

"Fine. Her disappearance, or whatever you call it." Mulder bounced his foot, since he couldn't pace. "We have information about the case."

"Take a seat." The cop gestured at two plastic chairs pulled up beside one of the desks. "I'll see if the detectives working it are around."

Mulder and Gimble sat down, but Mulder kept his eyes fixed on the officer with the mustache. What if nobody wanted to talk to them? That had happened to him more than once at the police station in Chilmark.

"He's talking to those guys by the vending machine," Gimble said. "Think they're the detectives?"

A tall man with squinty eyes, wearing a wrinkled button-down shirt with the sleeves rolled up, stood next to a short guy with a Santa Claus gut, wearing a fedora.

Laurel and Hardy.

"I know they are," Mulder said, hoping they hadn't noticed him at the crime scene. "I saw them at the cemetery."

Gimble's eyes went wide. "Did you talk to them?"

"No." Mulder watched as Laurel and Hardy approached.

"They don't look friendly."

The detective with the big gut spoke first. "We heard you have information about the Sarah Lowe case?" He flashed a badge. "I'm Detective Solano, and this is my partner, Detective Walker."

Mulder stood and wiped his sweaty palm on his jeans before he shook Detective Solano's hand. "My name is Fox Mulder."

Solano laughed. "I'm supposed to believe that's a real name?"

Gimble popped out of his seat. "I'm Gimble. I mean, Gary Winchester. I didn't see the body or anything, so you probably don't want to talk to me."

"The body?" Solano narrowed his eyes.

Mulder shoved Gimble out of the way before he opened his mouth again and dug a deeper hole for them. "What he means is, when I was jogging by Rock Creek Cemetery this morning, I saw the police cars and I stopped to see what was going on."

"Get to the part when you saw the body," Walker said.

"A detective unzipped the body bag, and that's when I saw the little boy."

Walker and Solano exchanged a look.

"That's the reason I'm here," Mulder rushed on. "I figured out there's a connection between Billy Christian's death and Sarah Lowe's kidnapping."

"Oh, you did? Why don't you enlighten us?" Walker sounded irritated.

This wasn't going the way Mulder had hoped. "In the picture of Sarah Lowe they showed on the news, she was wearing white pajamas with gray elephants on them. There was a stain right above the zipper." He pointed to the spot on his chest. "Billy Christian was wearing the same pajamas."

"You seem like a nice kid," Solano said. "And I'm sure you're trying to help. But do you know how many pairs of elephant pajamas there are in the world?"

"Lots," Walker added.

"I don't mean the same *style* of pajamas," Mulder said. "Someone dressed Billy Christian in the exact same pair that Sarah Lowe had on when she was kidnapped. The stain was the same shape and color, and it was in the same spot."

"Mulder notices that kind of stuff," Gimble explained. "He has a photographic memory."

Walker snorted. "Well, that changes everything. Can you predict the future, too?"

Solano laughed and his gut jiggled.

"This isn't a joke." Mulder raised his voice louder than he intended, and Detective Walker's expression changed from amused to angry.

"Get outta here." Walker pointed at the door. "We have real work to do."

Gimble grabbed Mulder's arm and tried to steer him toward the exit. "Come on. Let's go before they arrest us."

But Mulder didn't care. "The same person took both kids. Don't you want to catch him before Sarah Lowe ends up dead, too?"

Solano wiped his forehead with his sleeve and pointed at Mulder. "If we don't find that little girl, it'll be because of people like you. We already have dozens of bogus leads to follow up on, and every minute we're checking out a dead end is a minute we're wasting."

"But I'm not making this up." Mulder's shoulders sagged. "It's *not* a dead end."

"Stop talking," Gimble whispered.

A uniformed cop entered the building, leading a scrawny guy by the arm. The guy was barefoot and his hands were cuffed in front of him, below the cracked iron-on image of the Village People on the front of his T-shirt.

Solano nodded at the cop as he passed, then turned his attention back to Mulder. "Seems to me like you need an escort." He was reaching for Mulder's collar when pandemonium broke out in the precinct.

The scrawny guy in cuffs suddenly pulled away from the cop. He leaped up onto the nearest desk and shouted, "You don't have chains strong enough to hold me!"

The sergeant's office door swung open, and he surveyed the scene. "What the hell is going on out here? Get his ass down from there!"

"He's part of the head count from the PCP bust on Sixteenth Street," explained the cop who'd lost hold of the guy. "He thinks he's Superman."

The sergeant dragged a hand over his face. "I don't give a crap what he thinks. Get him down now."

"We need some help over here," the cop called out casually.

Why didn't he seem worried? Mulder had seen news reports about people high on PCP doing bizarre things like jumping through plate-glass windows because they couldn't feel pain.

"Your chains can't hold me," the junkie taunted again.

Several cops in street clothes surrounded the desk. "Come on down," one of them urged.

The junkie's eyes went wild. "You gonna jump me? Four

against one? While I'm cuffed? Not today, punks!" He raised his hands above his head and yanked his wrists apart.

Mulder heard the sickening crack of bones breaking, and the chain between the steel cuffs snapped. One of the junkie's wrists was at an unnatural angle, broken links of stainless steel hanging from the metal bracelets.

A cop winced and shook his head. "That's gonna hurt tomorrow."

"Did you see that?" Gimble looked stunned. "He broke his own wrist."

The junkie took off, jumping from desktop to desktop. Criminals cuffed to the desks cheered him on . . . right up until the moment when four cops tackled the guy and shoved him to the floor.

Detective Solano shooed Mulder and Gimble away. "Get the hell outta here."

"If you would just listen—" Mulder tried again.

Solano spun around. "I'm not asking anymore."

Gimble grabbed Mulder's sleeve and dragged him out of the precinct. "I'm not getting thrown in a holding cell with a guy who literally broke out of his handcuffs."

Mulder slumped against the wall outside, defeated. "The detectives haven't figured out the pajamas were the same, and they didn't believe me when I told them. I bet they won't even compare the photos to check."

"They're not going to find the little girl, are they?" Gimble asked.

"I'd be impressed if Solano and Walker could find their way out of a paper bag." Mulder kicked an empty brown bottle and watched it roll toward the parking lot.

"Maybe it's a sign you should stay out of this."

Usually nothing could quiet the constant storm that raged inside Mulder, but a sudden calm came over him.

"Or it's a sign that I have to find her myself."

CHAPTER 9

The next morning, Mulder's bedroom resembled the scene of a burglary. He had spent most of the night drawing and flipping through the books and papers scattered all over the floor—books about serial murder; Washington, DC, street guides; and the secondhand psychology textbooks he'd used in his campaign to get rid of the shrinks his dad forced him to see after Samantha disappeared. He had tossed his desk drawers in search of a sketch pad, which he ended up finding under his bed, and he spent hours drawing the dead bird with the arrows sticking out of its body. It wasn't the best drawing, but after several attempts, the bird didn't look like a pear with wings anymore.

Mulder kicked through a pile of clothes, in search of a clean pair of jeans and his favorite red T-shirt with the white stripes on the sleeves. A box of cereal hidden under a sweatshirt flew across the floor, scattering stale marshmallows on the carpet. But he hardly noticed.

Everything Mulder did, or didn't do, was to the extreme. He always had trouble sleeping, but often it turned into full-blown insomnia. After he watched his first Knicks game, he went to the library and read everything he could find about to the team. By the following week, he knew five seasons' worth of statistics. His father called these tendencies *obsessive*.

Mulder preferred *focused*.

And right now he was focused on finding Sarah Lowe.

The elephant pajamas were the only clue, and Billy Christian had been the last person wearing them. After downing two cups of instant coffee, Mulder skimmed last week's newspapers for details related to Billy Christian and the investigation, but he didn't find much. It was strange, considering how much information he found about Sarah Lowe. Her mother had shared the important details during the newscast, and journalists had covered the rest, interviewing everyone from Sarah's neighbors to her kindergarten teacher.

Why hadn't they interviewed Billy's teachers? Or his neighbors?

After digging through the pile of newspapers, Mulder finally found Billy's address in a tiny article in the *Washington Post*. He recognized the name of the neighborhood, and the lack of information suddenly made sense.

Mulder checked the address on the piece of ripped newspaper in his hand as he drove through Blue Hill. When he spotted Billy's house, he parked across the street. Blue Hill was one of the older neighborhoods in Northeast DC. The same Irish Catholic working-class families had lived here for generations—at least according to the guide on the Timeless Trolley Tour he'd taken right after he moved in with his dad. Mulder liked history, and he also liked knowing his way around.

Blue Hill was an insular community, and when a tragedy hit close to home, people in neighborhoods like that stuck together— and to one story. Mulder hadn't learned any of that from the trolley tour. Those were things you learned firsthand from living in a community like Blue Hill or Martha's Vineyard.

He stood on the sidewalk, looking at the Christians' modest home from across the street. The white house had black shutters and a small front porch, with a skateboard leaning against the railing.

Was that Billy's skateboard? Or did he have a sibling?

Mulder knew he couldn't just knock on the door and start asking questions. Billy's parents were probably still in shock.

But a little girl's life is at stake.

A screen door squeaked open behind him. An old lady wearing a flowered housecoat and pink curlers in her hair stepped onto the porch, eyeing him suspiciously.

"Good morning, ma'am," he said politely, hoping to put her at ease.

"That depends." She settled into a white rocking chair, watching him. "If you're a reporter, I don't want you standing in front of my house. And don't tell me that the sidewalk is public property, or I'll turn my dog loose on you."

Mulder liked the idea that he looked old enough to have a real job. Then again, maybe the old lady didn't have the best vision.

"I'm not a reporter. I'm a senior in high school."

She craned her neck to get a better look at him. "You don't live around here. I've never seen you before, and I know everyone."

He heard scratching on the other side of her screen door.

"I'm coming," the lady hollered at whatever was on the other side. It took her a moment, but she opened the door and a tiny orange puffball trotted out.

A Pomeranian? That was the dog she'd threatened to sic on him?

Mulder raised an eyebrow.

"She's meaner than she looks," the woman said defensively.

The puffball ran down the porch steps and straight to Mulder, yipping and wagging her tail. He bent down and scratched behind the dog's ears. The old lady seemed shocked.

"Do you have bacon in your pocket?" she asked, as if it were a perfectly normal thing to carry around.

"No, ma'am. Why?"

The lady clapped and the dog ran back up the steps. She scooped up the ball of fur and sat down in her rocking chair. "Gidget doesn't like strangers." Her logic was a little off, but at least she was talking to him.

Gidget sat up on her owner's knees like a tiny lion.

"She seemed to like me," Mulder reminded her.

"I noticed." She rocked for a moment, then added, "And Gidget is an *excellent* judge of character. Last year, the post office messed around with the routes and we got a new mailman. Gidget hated the man the first time she laid eyes on him. Three months later we found out he was stealing social security checks out of the mailboxes."

"My dad won't let me have a dog." Mulder wasn't sure why he said it, but it was true. He glanced at Billy's house.

Did Billy have a dog?

"Every child should have a dog," she said. "You keep looking at the Christians' house. Do you know the family? Or were you just curious?"

"Neither." Mulder stared at the sidewalk. Somebody had

traced a heart with two sets of initials in cement while it was still wet. "Someone kidnapped my sister when she was eight. I was home, too, but they only took her. So I know what it's like. I just wish there was something I could do."

"I'm sorry about your sister. Did the police find her—?" The old lady stretched out the word *her*, as if she'd caught herself before she said *her body*.

Mulder shook his head. "No. She's still missing."

The woman hugged her fur ball. "A child should be safe at home. It's bad enough that I can't walk Gidget outside after dark anymore without worrying about getting hit over the head. But after what happened to that sweet little boy, now I have to worry about a monster walking right through my front door."

He sucked in a sharp breath.

She can't mean . . .

"Is that what happened to Billy? Someone came into the house?" His heart pounded in his ears as he waited for her answer.

The old lady walked over to the railing and lowered her voice. "Billy's mother said the police didn't want to release too many details, because it would take longer to look into all the tips people were calling in."

Detective Solano had complained about following up on false tips and dead ends.

"But now that the little angel is gone, it can't hurt to tell you."

She hugged Gidget. "Billy's mother told me that he was playing on the living room floor with his Matchbox cars. The green one was his favorite," she added, as though she was sharing a secret. "The phone rang and his mom walked into the kitchen to answer it. She swore she wasn't gone for more than a minute or so. But when she came back, her baby was gone and the door was open."

Mulder's stomach bucked, and he almost puked. "The front door?"

She nodded, and the pink curlers jiggled. "That's right. Can you imagine? His mother called the police, and they arrived in less than five minutes, but there was no trace of Billy. I looked out the window when I heard the sirens."

"Do you remember what time it was?" His chest tightened.

"Must've been a few minutes before nine. I go to bed at nine o'clock on the dot every night."

The sidewalk seemed to shift under Mulder's feet. Billy Christian had been kidnapped from his home around the same time that Samantha and Sarah Lowe were taken. Even the details were eerily similar—all three children were eight-year-olds, playing in the living room just before they disappeared, and the front doors of their houses had been left open.

What if he was right and the same person was responsible?

Mulder had been so focused on finding a connection between Samantha's disappearance and Billy's and Sarah's abductions that he hadn't stopped to think about what it would *mean* if he found one. Mulder's throat burned and he stared at the sidewalk, blinking back tears as he processed the truth. He didn't want to be right anymore, because if he was . . .

It means my sister is dead.

CHAPTER 10

"What time did you say she was getting here?" Gimble asked Mulder for the tenth time. They were camped out at Mulder's apartment, waiting for Phoebe to show up.

"No clue. It depends on which airport she flew into." A piece of information he didn't know, because Phoebe had switched her flight to an earlier one without telling him until an hour ago, when she landed. Their conversation yesterday must have raised a red flag.

"I can't believe she just changed her flight and hopped on a plane." Gimble scooped some sunflower seeds out of the bag and alternated between crunching and talking. "That's hot."

"She always knows when I'm about to get myself into trouble,"

Mulder said, flipping through the worn paperback the Major had given him.

Gimble noticed. "You're actually reading *Stormbringer*? You must've been bored."

More like I needed a distraction.

"You said it was a good book. And I'd already watched the Knicks lose to the Clippers, 116 to 126. I figured the book couldn't be any worse."

Mulder didn't mention that before the game he'd spent most of the afternoon in the library, poring over microfiche, searching for articles about other missing children. If the person who killed Billy Christian and abducted Sarah Lowe was the same head case who had taken his sister, why the huge time gap? Or had the kidnapper taken other kids in between? Looking at photos of children who might never see their families again had left him feeling tense and edgy. He tucked the copy of *Stormbringer* in his back pocket.

"So what do you think?" Gimble asked.

"About the book?" Mulder shrugged. "I think all that stuff about keeping the balance between Law and Chaos is interesting."

"Me too. But don't tell the Major, or he'll want to talk to me about it nonstop." Gimble tossed some sunflower seed shells in the trash.

Mulder was impressed. His dad just left them all over the place.

"So back to your friend. Do you think she'll like me?" Gimble sounded genuinely concerned as he crunched the seeds.

The question annoyed Mulder. "I don't know. Why does it matter?"

"She sounded sexy on the phone. And if she looks half as good in person as she does in that picture in your wallet, I might propose to her."

Mulder instinctively touched his back pocket. "You went through my wallet?"

"You asked me to. The night you got pulled over for having a busted side mirror? Remember?" Gimble flicked the hair out of his eyes and broke into a grin. "So will she like me or what?"

"You're not Phoebe's type." Mulder sounded like a jealous boyfriend.

She wasn't his girlfriend or anything. Not that Mulder was opposed to the idea. He just didn't have the guts to bring it up. They had kissed a handful of times—okay, exactly five times—in the last two years, and one night after a party they had made out long enough to steam up the windows of the Gremlin and give Mulder something to daydream about for months. . . . Phoebe in jeans and a black bra, cheeks flushed and lips swollen from kissing him. But she didn't act like it was a big deal, and she didn't bring it up. So he didn't bring it up.

"I'll impress her with my wit and extensive knowledge of *Star Trek*. You'll see."

"Now I understand why you're so good at D and D," Mulder said. "You've got a great imagination."

Gimble was thinking of a comeback when the doorbell rang. Both boys spun around fast enough to give themselves whiplash. Mulder rushed to the door and flung it open.

Phoebe stood in the doorway, wearing flared jeans that looked cool instead of trendy on her; the gray-and-blue NASA T-shirt Mulder had given her two Christmases ago, which was an inch from becoming a full-fledged crop top; and sandals that crisscrossed over the tops of her feet, in tan leather that matched her skin tone. Her long blond hair was knotted just above her ears on either side of her head in Phoebe's version of Princess Leia buns, except Phoebe's were smaller and the ends of her hair stuck out of the center of each bun. Mulder couldn't tell if his best friend/girl of his dreams wore any makeup, but if she did, it wasn't much. A constellation of freckles spread over the bridge of her nose and spilled onto her rosy cheeks.

Phoebe planted her hands on her hips and opened her mouth to say something, but Mulder threw his arms around her neck before she uttered a word.

"I'm so glad you're here," he whispered.

She rested her palm against his chest, fingers splayed open, and gently pushed him back far enough to get a good look at him. "Of course you are. You look like a zombie."

Phoebe stepped around him and surveyed the living room.

She picked up the half-eaten bowl of cereal from the coffee table. Then she spotted a second bowl on the end table. "Is this all you've been eating?" She plucked two Hostess apple pie wrappers off the sofa and scrunched up her nose. "And don't lie, because I'll get the truth out of your Dungeons and Dragons–loving friend over there."

Gimble beamed at her. "You play D and D, too?" He turned and mouthed to Mulder, *I think I'm in love.*

Phoebe took another quick look around the room. "I take it your dad is on another one of his top secret trips?" She turned to Gimble. "And no, I don't play D and D. But I know how, and I speak Elvish."

Gimble brought his fist to his chest and let out a long breath. "It's like gods sent you down from heaven."

"How could you let him get this bad?" She glared at Gimble.

"It's not his fault," Mulder said. "I'm a big boy."

"So you claim." Phoebe marched down the hallway and peeked into each room until she spotted his open bedroom door. She walked in and shook her head in disgust.

Clothes were strewn all over the floor, along with books, sunflower seed shells, and more apple pie wrappers. Mulder scooped up an armload of clothes and dumped the heap in his closet.

Phoebe inspected his perfectly made bed. "Are you sleeping on the sofa again? Or did your insomnia come back?"

Mulder ran a hand through his hair. It was sticking up and he tried to smooth it down. "Sort of."

"*Sort of* to which one?"

He shrugged. "Both, I guess."

She picked up the book on his nightstand and read the title. "*The Meaning of Murder*? Doing a little light reading before bed? No wonder you can't sleep."

Gimble scanned the collection of serial killer books on Mulder's shelf and flipped through *Year of the Zodiac Killer*. "I love the Zodiac Killer."

"Do you know how disturbing that sounds?" Phoebe asked.

"I just meant that me and the Major—that's what I call my dad—we tried to crack the cryptograms the Zodiac Killer sent the cops," Gimble rushed on. "The authorities figured out three of the codes, and a high school teacher solved another one. But nobody ever deciphered the rest."

"Like I said, *disturbing*." Phoebe poked around the room, searching for more proof that he wasn't taking care of himself.

Mulder took the paperback out of his back pocket and dropped it on the nightstand.

Gimble looked through the rest of the *murder books*, as Phoebe called them. "So have *you* read all of these?"

"Uh . . . yeah." She held up the copy of *The Meaning of Murder*. "He made me read most of them, too."

"No one *makes* you do anything," Mulder said.

"True." Phoebe smiled just enough to make him remember what it felt like to feel her lips against his. She was like the sun—the bright spot in his universe, resisting the pull of the black hole that threatened to suck him in.

Why was she still hanging around with him? Guys tripped all over themselves to talk to her, even though most of them didn't understand half the things she said. Maybe that was the reason Phoebe hadn't found a boyfriend after he left. She didn't have a lot of options at a tiny island high school full of jocks.

But she will next year.

Mulder rubbed his eyes and tried to bury the thought. It was the beginning of April. Phoebe would be leaving for MIT in the middle of August. Less than five months—that was all the time he had left with her. Then she would meet a good-looking college genius and forget all about him.

"*Stormbringer?*" Phoebe noticed the green paperback on his nightstand. She skimmed a few pages.

"It's a fantasy novel the Major is obsessed with." Gimble didn't mention his mom.

"It sounds kind of weird." She flipped it over and looked at the cover.

"Everything about the Major is weird," Gimble admitted. "But it's actually a really popular book, and the author, Michael Moorcock, is a genius. The series inspired the alignment system in D and D."

"Is the guy on the front an elf?" she asked, referring to the male character with long white hair and alabaster skin, wielding a black sword.

Gimble gave her a strange look. "He's not an elf. He's an albino warrior from an alternate dimension."

"Of course." Phoebe tossed the paperback on the bed and took Mulder's hand, dragging him into the hallway. "Let's get you something to eat that doesn't come from the cereal aisle at the grocery store, while you fill me in."

Mulder nodded. He didn't have the energy to argue. His mind was reeling, and he couldn't stop thinking about the articles he'd found at the library this morning.

In the kitchen, Phoebe riffled through the cupboards while Mulder and Gimble sat at the table. She pulled out a loaf of white bread and jars of peanut butter and jelly. Then she placed slices of bread on the counter, assembly-line style.

"Start at the beginning, when you were jogging by the cemetery and you saw the body." She pointed a knife with a glob of peanut butter on the end at Mulder. "And don't leave out anything. You barely made any sense when you called last night."

Mulder took a deep breath, and for the next twenty minutes he described every last detail of the scene—the way Billy Christian's body was arranged on a bed of dead rose petals, with the black-and-white bird lying on his chest. The arrows sticking out of the bird's body that made it look like a cross between a compass and a medieval torture device. The white pajamas with the elephants, and the stain that reminded him of a hippo.

"Then I called you," he said finally.

Phoebe crossed her arms and her T-shirt rode up, exposing a wider sliver of skin. "That's it? You didn't do a single thing between last night and thirty minutes ago, when I showed up?"

Gimble coughed and looked away, as if he were the one being grilled, and Phoebe pounced on Mulder. "What are you leaving out?"

He shrugged. "I might have gone to the police station for a few minutes last night."

She balled up a napkin and threw it at him. "I told you to wait until I got here."

"I couldn't." Mulder pushed his chair away from the table and walked to the counter. He leaned over the sink and counted the water droplets in the aluminum basin. "I had to try."

"And let me guess. They didn't take you seriously?" she asked gently.

Gimble peeled the crust off what was left of his sandwich. "It was worse than that. They threw us out. Well, technically, they just kicked Mulder out."

"Anything else?" she asked, sensing there was more to the story.

Mulder scrubbed his hands over his face. Gimble already knew he'd gone to Blue Hill. Mulder had filled him in when

Gimble showed up at the apartment. Now he had to tell Phoebe. He couldn't hide anything from her—except the way he really felt about her. And he probably wasn't doing the best job at hiding that, either.

"I went by Billy Christian's house today," he admitted. "I wanted to tell his parents how sorry I was, but I couldn't do it."

Phoebe nodded. "That was a good call. His parents must be a wreck. To have someone find their child in a crypt, with a dead bird . . ." She hesitated. "It's so awful."

"I didn't even see them, but an old lady across the street told me about the night Billy was kidnapped." Mulder stalked around the kitchen. He couldn't stand still. His body buzzed with nervous energy. "He was playing in the living room when it happened. . . ." He stopped moving and looked Phoebe in the eye. "The person who kidnapped him just walked in through the front door."

"Fox . . . ," she warned.

"What are the odds?"

"It probably doesn't mean anything. You know that, right?" Her voice wavered.

"That's the same thing that happened to his sister," Gimble said.

Phoebe's eyes darted to Mulder.

"I told him."

Gimble frowned. "He had to tell me. I'm his best friend."

"His *second*-best friend." Phoebe jutted out her hip.

"You two can fight over me later. Right now I need your

combined brainpower and genius-level IQs," Mulder said. "I spent the afternoon in the library looking up articles about missing kids."

She shook her head. "Why would you do that to yourself?"

"Because I found six reports of children who disappeared from their homes at night, under what seemed like similar circumstances, in the past five years. Delaware, Rhode Island, Pennsylvania"— Mulder ticked off the states on his fingers—"Connecticut, Virginia, and Massachusetts. And I didn't include Wendy Kelly or my sister."

Mulder reached in his back pocket and took out the library card application he'd taken notes on. He didn't need the notes to recall the information, but he wanted to see the names of the kids and the dates they'd disappeared.

And the other dates.

His stomach clenched when he looked at them again. "These are the dates the kids were taken." He held up the paper so his friends could see it. "And these are the dates their bodies were discovered. Except for Daniel Tyler, who vanished six months ago from Cookstown, Virginia. The cops never found a body, so he could still be alive."

She closed her eyes for a second and took a deep breath before opening them again. "Did the article say anything about dead birds with arrows sticking out of their bodies?"

Gimble shook his head and shoulders like a wet puppy. "That's a *disturbing* thing to ask."

She glared at him. "It's a legitimate question."

"There was nothing in any of the articles about finding weird stuff with the kids' bodies, but you do the math." Mulder handed her the crinkled page. "The kids' bodies were found nine days after they disappeared, just like Billy's, which means the killer keeps them alive for eight days."

"A cult could be killing the kids," she said. "A group would explain the different locations."

Mulder didn't have that part figured out yet. "We don't have enough information to know for sure."

"But the police do," Gimble reminded him. "They've got photos of the body and the crime scene. Plus, they take notes."

"He's right," Phoebe said. "The case file would have all the details."

Mulder pressed the heels of his hands against his eyelids. "The detectives in charge of the case practically threw me and Gimble out of the station. There's no way they'll talk to us."

"Unless . . ." Gimble jumped out his chair. "So this one time, Theo—he's my dungeon master—he came up with a quest where I had to sneak into the royal castle and find out if the king was planning an ambush." He turned to Phoebe and puffed out his chest. "Gimble—my character in D and D—is a spy, so I do that kind of stuff all the time. But Gimble—my character, not me—doesn't have a high level of skill when it comes to doing stuff like scaling walls. But he's a level two—that's good, by the way—when it comes to deception."

"Did you really just say the words, 'my dungeon master'?" Phoebe rolled her eyes. "And I told you that I know how to play D and D. Is there a point?"

Gimble ignored her comment. He was too busy laying out his plan. "All we have to do is stake out the police station and wait until Detective Walker and Detective Solano aren't around."

"Or we could call the precinct and find out if they're on duty or not," Phoebe said.

"Or we do that," Gimble said, undeterred. "The point is, we'll wait until the detectives aren't there. Then we'll go in and say we're witnesses so we can get more information about the case."

"I tried that already, remember?" Mulder's mood was getting worse by the minute.

"You told them that you had information, not that you were an *eyewitness*," Gimble corrected him.

"What if they don't offer up anything?" Phoebe asked. "Detectives don't usually make a habit of telling potential witnesses the details about a case."

Gimble pulled an octagonal-shaped die out of his pocket. "Then we switch to diversion. Phoebe and I will distract the cop, which will give you a chance to get a look at the case file."

It wasn't the worst idea, and Mulder was willing to try anything.

Phoebe frowned. "Why do I have to help you distract the police?"

Gimble waved two fingers back and forth between them. "We speak the same language, like the Fonz and Pinky Tuscadero. You know?"

Phoebe looked at Mulder. "Do we need him? Because I might end up killing him before we get to the police station."

"You can't kill him," Mulder said as he led her out of the kitchen.

"Why not?"

Gimble scrambled behind them. "Lord Manhammer's Underground Strategy 101. Never kill the guy with the plan."

CHAPTER 11

Outside the Mulder Residence
10:30 P.M.

X sat in the black sedan, watching Fox Mulder and his merry band of fools. He had a decent view of the living room and kitchen, thanks to the sliding glass doors on the balcony. Not that it mattered. X was more interested in what the three kids were saying, and a few strategically placed bugs in the apartment allowed him to eavesdrop on their conversations. Unfortunately, there was no way to filter out the boring ones, like the one they were having now.

Fox and his friends had formulated a plan to go back to the police station what felt like hours ago, and ever since then X had been stuck listening to a lot of crap about a stupid game.

He almost regretted bugging the place.

This assignment was starting to feel like the organization's version of latrine duty. Nights like these made him second-guess his decision to turn down a job offer from the CIA two years ago.

At least the radio stations in DC were better than the ones in his backwoods hometown, a place he never planned to see again. He turned up "September," by Earth, Wind and Fire and closed his eyes.

The passenger door opened and X jumped.

"Sleeping on the job?" the boss asked, sliding into the seat next to him.

"I wasn't asleep."

"Sleep on your own time, and give me a report." A Morley dangled from the corner of the boss's mouth. "What has Fox Mulder been doing since the last time I saw him?"

"Plenty." X sat up straighter. "The kid's smart. I'll give him that much. Smarter than the DC police department, that's for sure."

"Details."

"Fox has been nosing around the Billy Christian case. The boy they found dead in the crypt."

"I'm familiar." Smoke filled the car with every word.

X couldn't understand how his boss managed to smoke and hold a conversation at the same time without dropping the ciga-rette out of his mouth. But as X's grandmother used to say, "The devil has his tricks."

"Fox thinks there's a connection between Billy Christian's and

Sarah Lowe's kidnappings. He claims the Christian boy was wearing the girl's pajamas when they found him. Fox noticed a distinctive stain."

"The boy has a photographic memory. Chances are, he's right."

"He tried to tell the detectives in charge of the case, but it didn't go well. He's planning to try again."

"So Fox Mulder is intelligent and persistent? Two qualities I value." A flicker of what X almost considered a smile pulled at the corner of the smoking man's mouth. "Let him follow this particular rabbit down the rabbit hole. Give him a little help if he needs it. I'm talking about a nudge, X. Not a push. I want to see how smart the boy really is."

"Understood."

"Good." The boss opened a pack of cigarettes and slid one out. He handed it to X. "You've never smoked before, have you?"

"I never had the urge."

The boss tucked the cigarette in X's shirt pocket. "Every man should try a Morley once in his life. Consider it a gift." As he stepped out of the car, he paused and turned to X. "And do try to stay awake. The work we're doing will change the world, and you have a front-row seat. If you aren't more careful, you'll miss it."

A chill ran up X's spine. The smoking man shut the car door and strolled off into the darkness, leaving X in a cloud of smoke.

The only trace his boss ever left behind.

CHAPTER 12

Mulder and Phoebe sat in the Gremlin under a streetlight in front of Gimble's house, waiting for him to put the Major to bed so they could leave for the precinct. Once the three of them had hatched their plan, Mulder couldn't wait to get going. But Gimble wasn't the holdup.

Phoebe had called the precinct earlier to find out if the Laurel and Hardy detectives were on duty, and their shift didn't end until ten. Mulder couldn't afford another run-in with them.

"What's taking him so long?" He tapped his thumb against the steering wheel.

"No idea," Phoebe said, changing the radio stations. She bypassed the Bee Gees and Toto and settled on Styx's "Renegade."

"You really are the perfect woman." Mulder smiled at her.

"I know."

Gimble's front door flew open and he ran down the sidewalk and stopped next to the car. The Major appeared in the doorway a second later, holding a mop across his chest like a firearm. "Get back in the house, Gary. This is a stage two lockdown."

Gimble cursed under his breath, then turned around and shouted, "I'm just warning Mulder."

The Major zeroed in on Mulder. "You need to get back to base, airman. They're coming. Soon they'll have all the bones they need."

Mulder stuck his hand out the window and gave the Major a thumbs-up. "Okay, sir."

"Who's coming?" Phoebe looked around.

"The aliens." Gimble sounded exasperated.

"His dad is a conspiracy theorist," Mulder explained.

"I picked up on that. Thanks." She craned her neck to get a better look at the Major.

"He's more agitated than usual," Gimble explained. "The cops found the body of a slumlord in Southwest DC. It's all over the news. The Major is calling him victim number five, and he wants me to find out if the man was missing any bones, even though the news is reporting that he hanged himself with a telephone cord."

"Why would your dad want to know if the man was missing bones?" Phoebe asked.

"He tracks crime and other weird stuff," Gimble said. "A

couple months back, he read an article about a woman who had been pimping out girls our age. The cops found the woman's body in a dumpster, and her hand was missing. The Major was convinced it meant something. Then a psychiatrist committed suicide, and the Major found out the guy was missing a bone in his foot. And that's how conspiracy theories are born."

"What's the theory?" Phoebe couldn't stop herself from asking. She had a little conspiracy theorist running through her blood, too.

"Do you really want to know? Because I feel stupid saying it out aloud." Gimble flicked his hair out of his eyes to avoid looking at her.

"Yes." She offered Gimble a sympathetic smile. "And you shouldn't feel stupid."

"Say that again in a minute." He sighed. "The Major thinks aliens are building a cyborg from a human skeleton."

Phoebe didn't bat an eye. "Do you think he knows the truth about Elvis?"

"Very funny." Gimble tried to sound annoyed, but his growing crush on Phoebe won out and he couldn't pull it off.

"She's not kidding," Mulder said. "She thinks Elvis is alive, hanging out in a small town somewhere, flipping burgers."

"Hardly. The King doesn't flip burgers. He's in a diner making peanut butter and banana sandwiches during the day and giving kids guitar lessons on the weekends." She waved at the Major, who responded by standing straighter. "I'd love to hear your dad's take."

"Gary William Winchester! Report to your senior officer immediately!" the Major roared.

"I'll be there in a minute!" Gimble screamed so loud that someone flipped on a light in the house next door. Then he turned back to his friends. "I can't go to the police station with you. The Major will be up all night adding junk to his stupid map and manning the telescope in case of an alien invasion."

"It's okay. You have to take care of your dad, and I have Phoebe to help me." Mulder felt sorry for his friend. The Major seemed like a lot of responsibility.

"Come by if you find out anything. I won't get any sleep tonight." Gimble tapped on the roof of the orange car. "Good luck."

Mulder pulled away from the curb. "We're going to need a lot more than luck."

Phoebe stopped Mulder outside the precinct door. "Forget diversion. We both go in there and say that we think we saw something the night Billy disappeared. Hopefully, one of us will get a chance to look at the case file or some notes."

"Sounds like a plan," Mulder said as they walked in. There was a reason he always went along with Phoebe's ideas. If she took one of those career tests that told you what kind of job you would be good at, Phoebe would get *criminal mastermind*.

Inside, the precinct was less intimidating than it had been the night before. Fewer people were cuffed to the desks, and nobody was standing on top of them, breaking their wrists to get out of handcuffs. Most of the cops were dressed in street clothes, with their badges hanging around their necks or clipped to their belts.

"This is way more real than I expected," Phoebe whispered.

"Are you chickening out?"

She punched him in the arm. "No. Are you?"

A cop in uniform with gray sideburns approached them. "You need some help?"

Phoebe stepped forward without hesitating. "We're here about Billy Christian, the boy whose body was found at Rock Creek Cemetery. We were both in the neighborhood the night he disappeared."

"Did you see something?" The cop glanced back and forth between them.

Mulder took over. "We think so."

"The detectives in charge of the case are off duty. Let me see who else is here." The cop looked around and spotted a young guy with brown feathered hair, wearing jeans and a *Battlestar Galactica* T-shirt. "Racca, I need you to take a statement," the cop called out to him. "These two might have information related to the Christian case."

"I'm on my way out." Racca sounded annoyed.

"This will just take a minute," the older police officer said, waving him over.

"He doesn't look old enough to be a cop," Phoebe whispered.

Mulder was thinking the same thing.

Then Phoebe noticed the guy's T-shirt and gritted her teeth. "Traitor."

Mulder tried not to laugh. "Some people like both *Star Trek* and *Battlestar Galactica*."

"It's an either-or situation," she said.

Officer Racca approached the other cop and gestured toward the door. "Wish I could help. But, like I said, I was just leaving."

"No, *Derek*. You *were* leaving." The older cop handed Racca a pencil. "And now you're staying. See how that works?"

Ouch.

Mulder felt bad for the guy.

Satisfied that he'd made his point, the older cop walked away, leaving Mulder and Phoebe with the awkward task of deciding whether they should make small talk.

"Come on back," Officer Racca said before Mulder thought of anything to say. He led them toward a cluster of desks on the opposite side of the room. He grabbed a stray chair and dragged it over to a desk piled high with crooked stacks of files. He flipped the chair around and slid it next to another one in front of the desk, and gestured at the empty chairs. "Sit."

Phoebe sat down next to Mulder, toying with the hair sticking out of her buns.

Officer Racca took a seat behind his desk, and the plastic hula dancer next to his phone jiggled. Pushing aside the mountain of manila folders, he reached for a white notepad and flipped to a new page. "So what have you got to tell me?"

"We saw a man hanging around in Blue Hill the night Billy Christian was kidnapped," Phoebe explained.

"Do you two live over there?"

"Yes, sir," Mulder said, watching him scribble something on the pad.

"What time?" the cop asked.

"About eight thirty." Phoebe didn't sound the least bit nervous.

He wrote down the information. "Let me get your names."

"Ellen Presley and Will Kirk," she said, without even a twitch of a smile. It was probably her only shot at sharing Elvis's last name.

But Will Kirk? Phoebe was putting a lot of faith in her either-or theory about *Star Trek* versus *Battlestar Galactica*. Mulder hoped Officer Racca wasn't a Trekkie.

"The man you saw . . . Can you describe him?" The cop didn't look up from the pad.

Mulder scanned the room. He noticed a hallway on the left side. Maybe the cops kept files and evidence down there?

Phoebe followed his gaze. "Actually, I got a better look at the man," she said. "He was your height, or a little taller."

"Excuse me, Officer Racca, but can I use the restroom?" Mulder asked.

Racca pointed with the end of his pencil. "Straight down that hallway. You can't miss it."

As Mulder walked away, Phoebe picked up where she left off. "Like I was saying, the man was about your height. . . ."

Mulder passed two cops hunched over a car magazine on one of their desks. He stared straight ahead, his heart pounding. It felt like everyone in the precinct knew he was up to something.

In the hallway, the fluorescent ceiling lights made him feel more exposed. He caught a glimpse of someone coming toward him—a tall man with an Afro and a bushy mustache, wearing black pants and a gray sharkskin button-down shirt. He couldn't see the man's badge, but he had a cool undercover-cop vibe.

"Looking for the bathroom?" he asked Mulder. "Fourth door on the right."

"Thanks." All the rooms Mulder passed were unmarked, and none of them had windows cut into the doors, so he couldn't tell if they were empty. The last thing he wanted to do was open the wrong door and walk in on a bunch of cops. The bathroom was a good place to plan his next move. He followed the curve of the hallway to the fourth door on the right, which was unmarked like the others.

The moment Mulder opened the door, he realized he wasn't in the restroom. He was standing in what looked like a war room—the place where Solano and Walker had laid out the clues and evidence related to the Billy Christian case. Photos of Billy, his parents, the family home, and the living room—the last place the boy was seen alive—were tacked on the wall along with files and handwritten notes.

One of the crime scene photos caught his eye. A shot of the body—Billy wearing Sarah's pajamas; the black-and-white bird, a magpie according to the label next to it, with eight arrows protruding from its body. A close-up revealed something Mulder hadn't seen before. An iridescent black stone rested inside the child's cupped hands, labeled NUUMMITE: METAMORPHIC ROCK.

Everything on the walls pointed to the occult.

And a serial killer.

The sound of footsteps in the hallway startled him. He couldn't stay in there long. He scanned the detectives' notes and the photocopied files on the wall, knowing he would remember them later. Words and phrases jumped out at him: *magpie, ritualistic, toxicology findings, arrows were carved from human bones.*

Mulder stared at the last phrase as if it were typed in a foreign language.

Human bones.

DISTRICT OF COLUMBIA
THOMAS SIXBEY, M.D.
CHIEF MEDICAL EXAMINER/CORONER

CASE REPORT

No. 86-431

Christian, Billy Barlow

The at-scene investigation included the following personnel:

The victim is a male, 8 years of age, identified as Billy Barlow Christian, who was reported missing on March 22nd. According to Christian's mother, the child disappeared from his home in Northeast Washington, DC. Mother reported leaving her son alone in the living room while she answered the phone. When she returned, her son was gone, and the front door was open (Case #22-915).

Victim's body was discovered on March 31, 1979, at 9:09 a.m., in Rock Creek Cemetery, inside a mausoleum (plot #1861). The victim was dressed in a pair of footed pajamas (mother noted they did not belong to the victim), and the body was arranged on a bed of dead rose petals (white), in a ritualistic manner. Child's hands were cupped, and he was holding a black stone (identified as nuummite, mineral native to Greenland). A small black-and-white bird was lying on the child's chest. Coroner identified the bird as a magpie. Bird's body was pierced with eight arrows, arranged in a radial symmetrical pattern.

Evidence collected at the scene includes the following:

1. 1 pair of size 8 footed pajamas, white with gray elephant pattern and 1 pair size 6 boys underwear
2. 3 bags of dead rose petals
3. 1 black iridescent stone identified as the mineral nuummite, roughly the size of a golf ball
4. 1 dead magpie
5. 8 hand-carved arrows

INVESTIGATOR: ___Edward Kurz___ DATE: March 31, 1979

DISTRICT OF COLUMBIA
THOMAS SIXBEY, M.D.
CHIEF MEDICAL EXAMINER/CORONER

AUTOPSY REPORT

No. 86-5011

CHRISTIAN,
I performed an autopsy on the body of ⇨ | BILLY BARLOW

at THE DEPARTMENT OF THE CHIEF MEDICAL EXAMINER/
CORONER , DISTRICT OF COLUMBIA on APRIL 1, 1979
                                            (DATE)
@ 1100 HOURS
     (TIME)
From the anatomic findings and pertinent history I ascribe
the death to:

(A)   CARDIAC ARREST

(B)   ACONITE POISONING

Other Significant Conditions: N/A

Anatomical Summary:

   I.   Stains on the inner forearms, with
        visible brushstroke pattern

   II. Ligature marks on both wrists

   III. High levels of alkaloids in the liver

   IV. Distended bladder consistent with
        toxicity

   Estimated time of death is between
   12:00 a.m. and 2:00 a.m. on March 30, 1979.

Upon initial examination at the scene, the body was stiff, indicating rigor mortis. No visible cuts, bruising, or other evidence of injury, but faint ligature marks were observed on both wrists.

Preliminary Toxicology Findings:

Victim absorbed a lethal dose of the alkaloids aconite and aconitine, through the dermis. Aconite and aconitine are naturally occurring toxins in the plant *Aconitum napellus* (monkshood), native to North America. Stains and stain pattern on the victim's forearms indicate a paste made from monkshood leaves was painted directly onto the victim's skin. The sedative Rivotril was also present in samples.

Forensic Notes:

Bird Carcass:

A bird carcass was found with the victim's body. Species was identified as a male Holarctic magpie, weighing 1 lb., 2 oz., with black-and-white feathers. The bird carcass was pierced with eight arrows, approximately .25 inches in diameter, arranged in a radial pattern.

The arrows were carved from human bones, belonging to adults.

OPINION:

Billy Barlow Christian, an 8-year-old white male, died of cardiac arrest, caused by ACUTE ACONITE POISONING.

_____
THOMAS SIXBEY, M.D.
CHIEF MEDICAL EXAMINER/CORONER

April 1, 1979

Internal and External Examination notes to follow.

CHAPTER 13

"What happened in there, Fox? You're scaring me," Phoebe said from behind the wheel of the Gremlin.

Mulder had managed to signal her from the hallway before he raced out of the precinct. After what he'd seen, there was no way he could've held up his end of the performance for Officer Racca.

Phoebe slammed her palm against the steering wheel. "Talk to me. Why are you so freaked out?" She looked around at the unfamiliar streets. "And where am I taking us?"

"I'm not sure. Just drive." His voice sounded shaky. "I opened a door thinking it was the restroom, and the evidence was tacked on the wall. Crime scene photos of Billy, with the dead bird on his chest. A label said it was a magpie."

Phoebe followed Dupont Circle and exited on Massachusetts Avenue. "I'm sorry you had to see those pictures."

"The close-ups were the worst. In the cemetery, I didn't have that much time to look at him." Mulder rubbed his eyes, wishing he could unsee some of the pictures. "There was other stuff, too. Notes, photos of Billy's living room, and an autopsy report. He was poisoned."

"Is that what has you so spooked?" Phoebe watched him in her peripheral vision. She knew Mulder too well for him to hide anything from her, and he didn't want to anyway. But he was having a hard time saying it out loud. The idea that he was investigating a serial killer was one thing. Knowing how sick that person actually was took the situation to another level.

"The arrows sticking out of the bird weren't made of wood." He hesitated.

"Okay? Are you going to tell me what they were made of?"

He gestured at the curb. "Pull over."

Phoebe found an empty space and parked. "Is this really necessary? I'm cool under pressure."

"Bones," he blurted out.

"What?"

"The arrows were made of human bones."

Phoebe stared at him, wide-eyed. "They weren't Billy's—?" She clapped her hand over her mouth.

Mulder took her hand and laced his fingers through hers. "No. They were adult bones."

"Only a psychopath would do that kind of thing."

Mulder heard the fear in her voice. "Now you're an expert on psychopaths?" he teased.

"I read your murder books. Remember?" Her shoulders relaxed a little. "Where do you think the killer is getting the bones?"

"The morgue, if I had to guess? Otherwise somebody would notice." Mulder's head buzzed, almost as if he could feel the synapses in his brain firing as the thoughts formed. He shot up in his seat. "Start driving. We need to get to Gimble's house."

"First it was *pull over*. Now it's *drive*. Are you aware that you have a problem making up your mind?" But she hit the gas and guided the car back onto Massachusetts Avenue. "Fox? That was a joke. What's going on in your head? Think out loud."

It's just a gut feeling. . . .

"What if the Major isn't as crazy as everyone thinks?"

Mulder knocked on Gimble's front door for five minutes before he heard someone shuffling around inside.

"They're probably asleep." Phoebe stood halfway down the brick steps that led up to the house.

"All the lights are on upstairs." He pointed at the second-floor windows. "And I hear someone."

The dead bolts clicked one by one, and Gimble poked his head out.

"Don't open it!" the Major shouted from somewhere behind him.

"It's just Mulder!" Gimble yelled back at the top of his lungs. "He has clearance, remember?"

"Sorry to come by so late," Mulder offered. "But you said you'd be up all night."

"He saw the crime scene photos," Phoebe added.

Gimble opened the door a little wider. "Get in here and tell me what I missed. And ignore the Major. He's having a rough night."

Mulder and Phoebe sat on the sofa and he recounted the story for the second time, while Gimble sat on the edge of the recliner hanging on every word. The Major stood at the window, with a mop propped against his shoulder like a rifle, watching the street—in case they had been followed.

"Arrows made of bones?" Gimble shuddered. "Gross."

The Major was talking to himself. "Anyone who tries to breach that door will find out what the soldiers of the 128th Recon Squadron are made of. Mark my words."

Mulder leaned over the arm of the sofa and lowered his voice. "Before we left for the police station, you said the Major thinks aliens are making a cyborg because some of the victims on his map were missing bones."

"Not *some* of them." Gimble's dad was suddenly standing behind the sofa where Mulder and Phoebe were sitting. "All of them."

"Do you have to sneak up on everyone?" Gimble asked, frustrated.

The Major raised his chin, with the floppy gray mop head resting on his shoulder. "You can take the man out of the air force, but you can't take the air force out of the man."

"Would you mind showing me your map again, sir?" Mulder asked.

"You're lucky you've got clearance, airman." The Major gave him a sharp nod.

When Phoebe stood up, the Major stopped in his tracks. "Not so fast, young lady. I'm afraid you'll have to stay here."

"Why? Because I'm a girl?" Phoebe narrowed her eyes and planted her hands on her hips. Her side buns had come loose and now she was left with two pigtails, but she still looked terrifying. "I speak three human languages, in addition to Elvish, and I know Morse code. I could've graduated from high school at fifteen, but I didn't want to go to MIT before I had a driver's license."

The Major opened his mouth to say something, but Phoebe

cut him off. "I'm also willing to bet that I'm the only person in this room, besides you, who knows how to fix an HT transceiver like the one you have over there." She pointed at the two-way radio on top of the TV set. "And I won the Massachusetts State High School Science Award two years in a row by demonstrating how the Big Ear telescope at Ohio State University intercepted the Wow! signal, and for a prototype I designed using applied robotics."

"Is she serious?" Gimble asked Mulder.

Phoebe's head snapped in Gimble's direction. "As a reactor operator at a nuclear power plant."

"I don't care if you're a man, or a woman, or a grizzly," the Major said. "You don't have security clearance, and no one is allowed access to my intel without clearance."

Gimble pretended to bang his head against the wall.

"Then how do I get clearance?" she asked.

The Major put down the mop. "You have to crack a code, and none of that easy stuff."

"Maybe she could take a quiz or something instead?" Mulder suggested.

"That's not the way I run my unit." The Major marched over to the shelves across from the sofa and returned holding a metal box. "Crack this and I'll grant you clearance."

"What's in there?" Mulder asked Gimble.

He shrugged. "No idea."

Phoebe took the box and opened it. She scrunched up her face and gave her friends a strange look. She flipped over the box and held up an object they all recognized. "A puzzle cube?"

"It's the only code the aliens can't crack," the Major said proudly, as if he had made the most significant discovery of the twentieth century.

"It's called a Magic Cube. You can't even buy them in the US yet." Gimble scowled at his father. "I told you not to go in my room."

"And whose contact got it for you?" The Major narrowed his eyes and pointed at Gimble like a drill sergeant. "Man up, airman, and support your unit."

Gimble crossed his arms and flicked his hair out of his eyes. "I get it back when she's done."

"All the squares on each side have to be the same color," the Major explained, turning to Phoebe. But she was already twisting the cube.

"Like this?" She held it up, each side a solid color. She tossed it to the Major, who stared at her with his mouth hanging open. "Now, let's see this wall."

After the Major recovered from the shock, he led them to the map, where he had added a new pin to Southwest DC.

"The woman pimping out those poor, innocent girls was the first target," he said. "She was missing her hand."

"She was a *madam*," Gimble told his dad. "We talked about this."

The Major frowned. "People called my grandmother 'madam.'

I will not insult her memory by referring to that evil woman the same way."

Gimble shook his head. "I give up."

His dad pointed at the newspaper clipping. "Says it right there. Third paragraph."

"What does it say?" Phoebe asked, craning her neck to get a closer look.

"The victim's body was mangled, leaving her right hand severed at the wrist," Mulder read. "And her hand was never found. According to a witness at the scene, there was blood everywhere, and bones were scattered all over the alley."

"The aliens tossed her around after they killed her, so no one would notice the missing bone," the Major explained.

The article confirmed his version of the story, except for the part about aliens. Not exactly the proof Mulder was hoping for, but the Major was just getting started. "Victim number two was the doctor. He almost slipped past me."

"But he wasn't missing a bone," Mulder pointed out.

"That's what I thought, too. Until I contacted my source at the morgue."

"Your what?" Phoebe blurted out.

"I installed a member of my unit at the county morgue, and he has friends in the same profession."

Gimble blew out a loud breath. "What he *means* is that one of the guys in his conspiracy forum happens to work there. His name is Sergio, and when he isn't checking bodies for missing bones, he lives in his mother's basement."

The Major gave Gimble a stern look. "Never judge a man by the size of his bank account or the place he hangs his uniform. Sergio risks his life for the mission. If the aliens found out that he's supplying intel that could expose their plan, they would take him out."

Gimble ignored his dad. "The psychiatrist was missing a foot bone."

"The second cuneiform," the Major added.

"Sergio wrote down the results of the autopsy report word for word on the paper bag that his burger and fries came in that day," Gimble said. "He mailed it to the Major's PO box."

Mulder shrugged. "Sounds official enough to me."

"So the psychiatrist is a strong *maybe*," Phoebe said.

The Major provided them with the details on other less-than-stellar citizens—a guy selling moonshine in the woods who was missing plenty of bones after he was supposedly attacked by wild animals, a drug dealer who was missing a piece of his jawbone after he was beaten to death (according to the newspaper), and a bookie who was missing a bone in his arm (according to Sergio).

Mulder knew Gimble's dad wasn't someone most people would consider a reliable source, but the man spent every day holed up in the house, scouring the papers and the news, looking for connections and patterns.

"And that brings us to the slumlord who supposedly hanged himself with a telephone cord," the Major said. "The aliens took his finger."

Phoebe squeezed past Mulder so she could read the article. "This one is legit, for sure. The police assumed a disgruntled tenant chopped it off."

"But the guy hanged himself," Mulder said.

"That's what the aliens want you to think." The Major swiped something from between a stack of newspapers on the floor and handed it to Mulder. A black-and-white crime scene photo.

Gimble realized what Mulder was holding and turned to his father. "Where did you get that?"

"Sergio took it from the coroner's office when the morgue sent him to pick up the body."

"You and Sergio could get in serious trouble for doing something like this," Gimble warned.

The Major scoffed, "We're at war with extraterrestrials. Do you think I'm afraid of the police?"

Mulder studied the grisly photo of the man dangling from a ceiling fan. "What am I looking for, sir?"

"Have you ever rigged a boat, airman?" the Major asked.

"Uh . . . no, sir."

"I bet the man swinging from that telephone cord in his big-city apartment hadn't, either."

Gimble moved closer, suddenly interested. "Where are you

going with this?" It was the first time Mulder had seen him take his father seriously.

The Major pointed at the knot above the noose. "That's a sheepshank knot. Sailors use it for rigging."

Gimble stared at his father in awe. Mulder and Phoebe were blown away, too.

"I was damned surprised when I saw it myself," the Major continued. "I would've expected the aliens to go with something simpler, like a good old-fashioned slipknot."

"Maybe you can give them lessons," Gimble said. "And teach them to make macaroni and cheese while you're at it."

Mulder tuned everyone out and studied the wall—molecular formulas and geometric sequences, next to a coupon for rug cleaning and a secret message the Major had "decoded" from the back of a cereal box. A conspiracy theorist's map and extensive knowledge of sailing knots wouldn't be enough proof for the police.

Mulder shook his head, frustrated. "We'll never convince the detectives that whoever murdered the people on the Major's wall is the same man who killed Billy."

"What makes you so sure the killer is a man?" Phoebe never passed up a chance to challenge him. It was one of the things he loved about her.

"There have only been six female serial killers in America. I looked it up," Mulder countered. "I was going with the odds."

"Six they've *caught*," she couldn't resist adding. "But I'm not so sure it's the same person. According to your murder books, serial killers don't usually change the type of victims they select over-night and go from kidnapping children and stuffing them into crypts to murdering adults and stealing their bones."

She had a point.

Mulder did a mental run-through of what he knew about serial killers, which extended beyond what he'd learned from *The Meaning of Murder*. After Samantha disappeared, researching crime and psychology became kind of a weird hobby. At the time, Mulder hadn't given much thought to *how* weird. He just added it to his growing list of interests—the New York Knicks and basket-ball, *Star Trek* and the NASA space program, Farrah Fawcett and Wonder Woman, and kidnappers and serial killers.

Initially, he had focused—or *fixated*, as Phoebe called it—on kidnappers. But serial killers, like David Berkowitz (known as Son of Sam), John Wayne Gacy, and Ted Bundy had been all over the news for years now, and with Mulder's memory, things stuck.

"Maybe the killer isn't changing his victimology," Mulder said, thinking out loud. "If the arrows are part of his signature, then he needs to get the bones from somewhere."

Phoebe nodded, as if she understood what he meant, but Gimble was lost.

"What's a signature?"

"It's a calling card—something unique the killer leaves behind at the crime scene," Mulder explained. Gimble stared blankly at him, so Mulder came up with an example. "After the Boston Strangler murdered his victims, he took whatever he used to strangle the victim and tied it in a bow around the person's neck."

"Like the missing bones," the Major said, picking up the tail end of the conversation. "That's the aliens' signature."

"Thanks for that, Major." Gimble craned his neck and looked over at the window, in an obvious move. "Is it safe to leave that post unmanned?"

The Major's gaze darted to the window. "Don't worry, airman. I've got eyes on it." But his paranoia won out a moment later, and he marched back to the window.

Phoebe shook her head at Gimble. "That was mean."

"Say that after you've spent twenty-four hours with him," Gimble said, then turned to Mulder. "Even if it's part of the signature, stabbing a bird with anything and then making a symbol with its dead body sounds like part of a satanic ritual."

"It's so sick." Phoebe wrapped her arms around her stomach and cringed.

"And Billy Christian's body was found in a crypt," Mulder added.

"Don't forget about the mummy stone," Gimble reminded him.

"It's called *nuummite*," she snapped, suddenly on edge.

She's not the only one, Mulder thought.

Walking into the wrong room at the police station and sneaking a look at the photos and the reports had been dumb luck, and he knew it. There were still so many missing pieces. "We need more information about the stone and the poison. We should hit the library tomorrow morning and see what else we can find out."

The sound of footsteps and rustling attracted everyone's attention. The Major had left his spot by the window and was racing around the room, opening boxes and pulling books off the shelves.

"Is he okay?" Mulder asked.

Gimble sighed. "The occult talk probably agitated him."

The Major rushed to his recliner and lifted the seat cushion. He returned clutching a paperback copy of *Stormbringer* against his chest like a teddy bear. "The human race violated the principles of Law and upset the Cosmic Balance. That's why the aliens chose us to be their guinea pigs, and they won't stop until they achieve their goal." He pointed at a DNA chain drawn on the wall. "The aliens want to experiment on us, and manipulate and distort our genetic code. Until the Cosmic Balance is restored, we're at their mercy."

"Okay, time for bed. Nobody wants our DNA," Gimble said, steering his father toward the staircase. "You need some sleep."

"We should go. I think we upset him," Phoebe whispered to Mulder, and then headed for the door.

"Okay." Mulder took another look at the Major's morbid collage before he followed.

The Major darted in front of Phoebe, blocking her path. "Take this." He thrust the copy of *Stormbringer* at her.

"I couldn't—" she started.

"Just take it." Gimble yawned and rubbed his eyes. He looked exhausted. "He's not going to let you leave without it."

Phoebe accepted the tattered paperback. "Thanks."

"Things aren't always what they seem." The Major stared at her, his expression grim. "A skilled puppet master never lets you see the strings."

CHAPTER 14

Phoebe talked nonstop the whole ride back to Mulder's apartment, arranging and rearranging the information they had uncovered. "I'm giving you permission to make fun of me after I say this, because it's the kind of thing you hear in lame horror movies. But I still have to say it."

"Go ahead." Whatever she was about to tell him couldn't be worse than the mental train wreck in his head.

"I have a bad feeling about all this. There, I said it."

"Do you feel better?"

"No." She hugged her knees, balancing the wooden heels of her Dr. Scholl's sandals on the edge of the seat. "The person who killed Billy is a sick bastard, but he's also evil. Like Charles Manson and Son of Sam evil."

"Maybe you should stop reading my murder books?" He looked over at her. "They'll give you nightmares."

"Then why do you read them?" She caught herself. "Because you don't sleep."

Mulder parked the car and smiled at her. "You're pretty smart for—"

"For *what?*" She narrowed her eyes.

"For someone who believes that Elvis is still alive, making sandwiches at a diner."

"You're trying to distract me because you think I'm scared." She got out of the car and stayed a step ahead of him as they walked to the apartment.

"That's not it," Mulder tried to tell her, but she ignored him. He paused at the door and looked at her. "You're not the person I'm trying to distract."

"Fox—"

The phone rang inside the apartment, and Mulder fumbled with his house keys.

"Who's calling so late? Your dad?"

"He almost never calls." When Mulder finally got the door open, he jogged to the kitchen and picked up the receiver. "Hello?"

"Fox?" his mom cried out, the way she used to when he wandered away from her in the grocery store.

"Mom? Are you okay?" His insides knotted.

She burst into tears. "Where have you been? It's the middle of the night."

"I was at my friend Gimble's house." He didn't remind her that he was almost eighteen.

"I thought . . ." She sniffed, and his chest tightened. "I thought I'd lost you, too."

He swallowed the fist-sized knot in his throat. "I'm fine, Mom. You're not going to lose me. Phoebe's in town, remember? I was introducing her to my friend, that's all."

His mom blew her nose on the other end of the line. "I'm acting ridiculous. It's not even that late for you. I tried to call your father, but he was 'unavailable.'"

Mulder leaned his arm against the wall and pressed his forehead into the crook of his elbow. "Dad is always unavailable. You know that."

Phoebe touched his arm, a silent show of support.

"You're right." His mom sounded like herself again. "I just need some sleep."

"I'm sorry that I worried you, Mom." The guilt he fought so hard to keep at bay threatened to crush him.

"Good night, honey. I love you."

"Love you, too. Night." Mulder waited for her to hang up, keeping the phone against his ear until the line went dead.

Phoebe took the receiver out of his hand and returned it to the cradle.

Mulder's heartbeat thumped in his ears, and a familiar burning sensation spread through his chest. Samantha had been missing for almost five and a half years, and his mom still felt the effects of that loss every day. She never admitted it outright, but she didn't have to, because he felt the same way.

Phoebe wheeled him around and took his face in her hands. "Your mom is fine. Don't torture yourself."

"I'm not." He tried to turn away, but she kept her palms firmly planted on his cheeks.

"And don't lie to me."

"I'm not trying to torture myself, but I can't stop thinking about what happened." He fought to keep his voice steady. They both knew he was talking about the night his sister vanished.

"When was the last time you slept?"

He shrugged.

Phoebe closed her eyes for a second and took a deep breath, and Mulder finally got out of his own head long enough to look at her. She was beautiful. Her long lashes brushed her cheeks, and her full bottom lip made it look like she was perpetually pouting—or trying to seduce him. Not that it would take much effort on her part. He had a dozen issues of *Playboy* magazine stashed under his bed, and if he had a choice between any of the women on those pages and Phoebe, he would choose the girl standing in front of him.

Phoebe's eyelids fluttered as her eyes began to open. Mulder's whole body was on fire now, and his heart ached so damned bad. Her lips always took the pain away, even if the aftermath of their kisses caused him a different kind of pain.

He stopped thinking and pressed his lips against hers. Her lips parted, and she sighed softly.

Mulder slid his hands down her sides and cupped her ass.

"Fox?" she murmured.

Hearing her say his name in that breathless voice drove him half crazy. They stumbled to his room, Mulder walking her backward down the hallway, his mouth never leaving hers. His elbow hit the doorjamb on their way in, but the sting only made everything inside him burn hotter.

As he eased her onto the bed, she put her hand against his chest, holding him back. "I know why you're doing this."

Mulder stared into her big blue eyes. "No, you don't."

Because I'm too scared to tell you how I feel.

She was still out of breath, and her chest rose and fell faster than normal. "Kissing me won't make you forget."

"I don't want to forget. I want to find the psycho who took my sister."

"But the person who's taking these kids might not be *that* person." She searched his face. "You know that, don't you?"

"Not until I find him."

"Fox—"

"If there's even the slightest chance the same thing happened to Samantha, I have to know," he said.

Phoebe gave him the same sad look he remembered from the day he moved. "Promise me you won't get obsessed with this. That you'll be careful."

Mulder moved closer. "I promise," he said with his mouth against hers. Then he kissed her until their lips were swollen and they were both exhausted.

Phoebe nuzzled his neck and he tightened his arm around her waist, listening to her breath against his ear. Holding her made him feel normal, as if he were just another guy who loved playing basketball and hanging out with his friends. A guy who was still trying to figure out the big stuff—like where he should go to college in the fall and how to ask the girl he'd kissed five minutes ago out on a real date.

Hours later, when the first blue-black signs of dawn began to bleed into the sky, Mulder was still awake. The urge to kiss Phoebe and feel her lips against his was replaced by a different urge. It compelled him to ease out of bed without disturbing her and cross the room to open the closet door.

He took a marker off the shelf and picked up the yardstick he had dragged from Martha's Vineyard with him to DC. It was the yardstick his mom had used to record Samantha's height every year on his sister's birthday. Mulder flipped it over to the back, where he was keeping a record of his own.

He wrote a number above the one he had recorded yesterday.

1,952

The number of days since the last time he'd seen his sister.

CHAPTER 15

Lauinger Library, Georgetown University
April 2, 10:40 A.M.

Mulder woke to the sound of the shower. He rolled over and stared at the wrinkled sheets next to him. He could still see the faint outline of the spot where Phoebe had slept last night.

The fact that she was already out of bed and in the shower saved him from the awkward moment when she would inevitably tell him why something like this couldn't happen again.

He tugged on a pair of jeans, threw on a plaid button-down, and rolled up the sleeves. He padded down the hallway, getting his ass kicked by his thoughts, so he didn't notice the bathroom door open. Phoebe walked out, and he almost plowed into her.

Mulder caught her by the shoulders. "Sorry. I wasn't paying attention." Phoebe was wearing a flowered peasant top with jeans and her wooden Dr. Scholl's sandals, and he let his fingers linger on her bare skin.

"That's a first," Phoebe teased. She had a deeper voice than most girls, and it sounded even sexier in the morning. Her damp blond hair framed her face, and her expression made him want to kiss her again. She tilted her head to the side, a sign she was weighing her options.

Did that make *him* an option?

"I wanted—" he started to say, just as she said, "About last night—"

So much for dodging an awkward moment.

"What were you going to say?" she asked, her expression hopeful.

"'My tongue gets tied when I try to speak,'" he quoted with a sheepish smile. "You go ahead."

Suddenly, Phoebe seemed nervous. She parted her hair down the middle, gathered one section, and pulled it through a hairband to make a pigtail. "I know the situation with Sarah Lowe is stirring up all sorts of memories and emotions, and I'm here for you." She finished twisting one side and moved on to the other one, her fingers moving faster now. "But I can't be your security blanket whenever you get lonely."

"That's *not* how I think of you," he blurted out. And it wasn't.

A security blanket?

Suddenly, it hit him.

He only had the guts to act on his feelings for her when life got intense. The rest of the time he was too paralyzed to make a move, or admit the way he felt. Why *wouldn't* she think that he was only interested when he got lonely?

"I'm a jerk, Phoebe." Mulder ran his hands over his face. "That's not the way I feel about you, at all."

She was watching him. "Then how *do* you feel?"

Tell her the truth.

Tell her that you think she's the smartest person you've ever met. The only person who knows more about Star Trek *and rocket science than you. Who knows that you never sleep in your bed, unless she's in it. Tell her every time she smiles, you wish that you were her boyfriend.*

Mulder rehearsed the words in his head, but he couldn't get them out.

The stakes were too high with Phoebe. He couldn't risk losing his best friend if she didn't feel the same way, even though he was pretty sure she did. And what if she had real feelings for him, too? He couldn't hurt her, the way he seemed to hurt everyone else he cared about.

No way.

Phoebe deserved better. No. She deserved the best.

And I'm not even close.

Mulder's eyes locked on hers, and he tried to find the right words. He took a deep breath, even though he had no idea what he was going to say. "Phoebe, I—"

The doorbell rang and they both jumped.

Who's here this early?

He cleared his throat to start again, but the doorbell rang two more times.

Phoebe sighed. "Maybe you should see who it is?"

"Right," he said, stepping around her.

The moment was over. Whoever was at the door had probably saved him from total humiliation or losing his best friend.

Mulder opened the door, and Gimble pushed past him. "What took you so long?" he asked, unzipping his blue velour track jacket.

"How did you get here?" Mulder asked.

The Major refused to get Gimble a car. He was convinced that someone would plant a tracking device on it and use it to locate his base of operations.

"I took the bus." Gimble strolled into the kitchen and opened the refrigerator, something he couldn't do at home without removing a bike lock. He popped the tab on an orange soda and took a swig.

"I said I'd pick you up," Mulder reminded him.

"The Major blew a gasket when he found out I plugged in the phone upstairs. It's only for 'life-or-death emergencies.'" Gimble moved on to the pantry and rummaged around until he found a Hostess cherry pie. He ripped open the wrapper and took a bite. "I didn't feel like manning the telescope all day, watching for little green men. So when he locked himself in the basement early this morning to work on his files, I wrote him a note and bailed."

Phoebe walked into the kitchen as if everything was perfectly normal. But Mulder noticed that she didn't look at him.

Because she cares? Or because she doesn't?

She plucked the pastry out of Gimble's hand. "I hate to interrupt such a nutritious breakfast, but the library opens in ten minutes. You can eat in the car."

"Whatever you say." Gimble flashed her a smile and headed for the front door.

Mulder hung back and caught her hand as she started to walk away. "Phoebe? Wait."

She turned and locked eyes with him, and his stomach bottomed out.

He had to explain and make her understand. "I don't want—"

"That's the problem, Fox. You don't know what you want." She smiled enough to let him know everything was okay.

Except it wasn't. Not for him.

"I hope you figure it out one day so you can finally be happy." Phoebe squeezed his hand, and then she let go.

"We didn't have to come here," Phoebe said, eyeing the Gothic architecture surrounding the quad. "Georgetown isn't the only university in DC with a library."

"But I know this one is open to the public," Mulder said. He remembered the detail from the campus tour he'd taken with his dad, back in October.

"Why does it seem like I'm always missing something?" Gimble asked.

"Because you are." Phoebe flashed him a wicked smile, the tips of her blond pigtails grazing her shoulders as she walked.

"Don't look so proud of yourself. I set myself up for that one." Gimble ducked under the limb of a massive oak and turned to Mulder. "So what's the story?"

"Fox's dad wants him to go to Georgetown," Phoebe explained, sharing another piece of information that Gimble didn't know.

"And you're not into it?" Gimble asked.

Mulder shrugged. "I can't picture myself here."

Georgetown was for guys who wanted to graduate and go into politics or law, and join country clubs. Guys like him, who wanted to travel into space or invent a teleportation device so Scotty could "beam them up," went to schools like MIT, Berkeley, and Cornell.

"Did you decide where you're going yet?" Mulder asked Gimble.

"The Major thinks I'm joining the air force. He writes a letter to the Air Force Academy every week. Then he folds up the letter until it's the size of a stick of gum, hides it in the bottom of an empty cereal box, and throws the box away when he takes out the trash."

Phoebe reached up and plucked a pink cherry blossom off a tree as she passed. "Is he confusing the garbage can with the mailbox?"

Gimble stared at his blue-and-red-striped sneakers, and his hair fell forward, shielding his face. "That would be too normal. He thinks Sergio retrieves his gum-sized letter, covered in cereal crumbs, and delivers it to the superintendent of the academy."

"What are you going to tell your dad?" Phoebe sounded concerned.

Gimble shrugged. "Nothing until I find out if Virginia Tech or one of my backup schools offers me a scholarship. Then I'll convince him that I'm in a program studying top secret alien technology."

"Are you sure this is the way to the library?" Mulder asked.

The black hole that lurked in the darkness, waiting to drag him into oblivion, felt closer than usual. Based on the information he'd gathered at the public library about the other missing kids, the killer would keep Sarah Lowe alive for only four more days.

What if no one found her in time?

Gimble rotated the campus map in his hand until it was right side up. "The Lauinger Library should be behind the old library over there." He pointed at the far end of the quad.

They passed a group of guys wearing Georgetown Crew T-shirts with gym bags slung over their shoulders. Two girls giggled and flirted as they walked beside them, their sorority letters prominently displayed across their chests.

Phoebe narrowed her eyes. "When I get to MIT, I'm starting a sorority for girls who know more about splitting atoms and hydraulic energy sources than lip gloss. If they can't run through the periodic table of elements like it's the alphabet, they'll get cut."

Gimble turned around so he was walking backward as they moved between two buildings. "Instead of Greek letters, you can put the symbol for francium on your shirts. It's the most un—"

"Unstable element on the periodic table, with a half-life of twenty-two minutes at its most stable," Phoebe finished for him. "I like it. And we'll throw the best parties, because all the drinks we serve will produce cool physical reactions, like nitro cocktails and dry ice martinis."

Mulder wondered if Gimble realized she was serious. Some people spent lots of time talking about all the cool things they planned to do, but Phoebe actually went out and did them.

When Mulder was younger, he believed that anything was possible. Before his dad told him that he couldn't be an astronaut. Before Samantha vanished.

What was he supposed to believe in now? Brutal memories and broken families? Unanswered questions and unhappy endings? Numbers on a yardstick in his closet?

Other people moved on after tragic events, but he wasn't one of them. Moving on meant giving up on his sister. Accepting that she might never come home and finding a way to live with it. And he wasn't capable of doing those things.

A sudden breeze shook the branches of a cherry tree, and pink blossoms fluttered through the air and settled on the grass. Mulder wondered if he'd ever be able to look at flower petals again without picturing Billy Christian's eight-year-old body lying on top of a bed of them.

Phoebe stopped walking and scrunched up her nose. "Is that it?"

The building at the end of the sidewalk was a solid mass of concrete, modern and utilitarian compared to the detailed Gothic architecture that surrounded the quad.

"It's like someone played that *Sesame Street* game 'One of these things is not like the others,'" she added.

"It doesn't matter if it's ugly, as long as it has the books we need," Mulder said, taking the steps two at a time.

He held the door open for Phoebe, and let go before Gimble made it through.

His friend caught it and followed them. "Real funny. I'm going to tell the Major that you want him to tell you more about the cyborg the aliens are building."

"While you're at it, ask him about Elvis," Phoebe said.

Inside, the building stretched skyward, with floor after floor of narrow shelves facing the railings and the lobby. Students were crammed beside one another, scouring the shelves.

"It's claustrophobic in here," Gimble whispered.

"Think of it this way," Phoebe said. "The sooner you find the information we need, the faster we're out of here."

"Or the faster *you* find it," Gimble shot back. "This is a team effort, Phebes."

Mulder cringed as if he were the one about to face Phoebe's wrath. Then he did what any best friend would do and took off for the circulation desk.

Just before he was out of earshot, he heard Phoebe say, "Have I ever told you how I feel about cutesy nicknames, *Gims?*"

Mulder approached the desk and waited for the librarian to notice him—if the woman wearing a pastel-pink V-neck sweater and a macramé choker sitting behind it was actually the librarian. She stood out in the sea of Hoya sweats and preppy collared shirts with alligators on the pockets.

She looked up from the stack of library cards she was stamping. "May I help you?"

"Yes. I'm looking for books about magpies, metamorphic rocks, and . . ." He lowered his voice. "Aconite poisoning."

The woman didn't bat an eye. She was definitely the librarian. "That's an interesting combination. Some scholars believe the Roman emperor Claudius was poisoned with aconite." She stood and came around the desk. "Come with me, and I'll point you in the right direction. Are you researching Claudius or just the poison?"

Mulder coughed and followed her toward a narrow staircase. "I'm researching deadly plants." That sounded plausible.

Gimble and Phoebe caught up to them, and Mulder gestured in her direction. "And my friend is writing a paper about meta-morphic rocks."

"Minerals, actually," Phoebe said. "Everything from the physical properties to new age stuff, like crystal healing and—"

"Magic spells," Gimble added.

The librarian paused on the third-floor landing and gave Gimble a curious look. "Are you interested in alchemy?"

Phoebe swooped in. "He plays Dungeons and Dragons."

The librarian started to ask a question but changed her mind. "Here we are," she said, leading them to the stacks on the third floor.

Phoebe stood at the railing and peered down at the floors below and then at the ones above. Despite the fact that the layout forced people to squeeze past one another as they searched the shelves, the view was impressive.

"Birds are over here." The librarian ran her finger along the side of the shelves to indicate where to look. "And minerals and crystals are over here in the five hundreds."

After the librarian pointed Phoebe in the right direction, she told Mulder, "We need to go up to the fourth floor to find what you're looking for."

"Okay." He signaled Phoebe. "Grab Gimble when you finish, and let's meet up in the study rooms."

"They're on the top floor," the librarian added.

After the librarian showed Mulder where to find books on aconite and historical figures who were poisoned—cleverly titled *Lessons in Poison: Historical Figures Who Died from Common Poisonous Plants*—Mulder pulled every text he could find that mentioned monkshood and wolfsbane, the common names of the plant that produced aconite.

It took him a few minutes to make his way up to the top floor. He had to inch his way past the students gathered at the shelves facing the center atrium. He spotted Gimble and Phoebe in one of the rooms, sitting at a table piled with books.

"You made it," Gimble said as Mulder opened the door.

"Poison is a popular subject," he said, dumping the texts on the table. "What's the game plan?"

"I must've heard you incorrectly. Are you suggesting we need a *plan?*" Phoebe gave him an incredulous look. Mulder didn't make plans, unless they involved acting on his impulses and strategizing at the last minute. She seemed like herself again, but he couldn't forget last night that easily.

"Just this once," he said, trying to put on a good act. "But don't get used to it. I'm switching back to the unpredictable guy who makes snap decisions as soon as we walk out of here."

She ignored him. "I'm already taking notes on nuummite, and you should cover aconite since you saw the autopsy report."

"Why do I get stuck with birds?" Gimble complained. "I want poison or volcanic rocks. Birds are lame." Phoebe opened her mouth to respond, and Gimble backtracked. "Forget it. I'll take birds."

"I love it when we all agree." She returned her attention to the volumes open in front of her.

Within minutes, Mulder's friends were madly taking notes, while he breezed through his pile of books. He didn't need notes. Even without a photographic memory, it would've been easy to remember the information. It was straight out of an Agatha Christie novel.

Mulder leaned back and stared up at the perforated ceiling squares.

"Anything interesting?" Gimble asked.

"It depends. Do you want to poison an emperor or harpoon a whale?" Mulder shut the last book and pushed it away.

Phoebe looked up from her notes. "What have you got?"

"Aconite comes from the monkshood plant, and it's one of the oldest poisons in history. 'The mother of all poisons'—that's what one of the books calls it. It dates back to the twelfth century BC, and cultures all over the world used the stuff." He rattled off the facts, his volume increasing to match his frustration. "In ancient

China they used aconite to make poison darts, aboriginals in the North Pacific coated harpoons with mashed-up monkshood leaves to hunt whales, and the Greeks and Romans poisoned their enemies with it."

"Fox? Why are you getting so upset?" Phoebe asked.

Mulder ignored the question.

"Forget the whales," Gimble said. "Will the aconite help us track down the killer?"

Mulder pushed his chair away from the table and stood up. "No. Because monkshood grows all over North America. The killer could have it in his backyard."

"Are there different species? Maybe that would narrow it down," Phoebe suggested.

"I doubt it matters. Aconite is a toxic compound in all of them." Mulder stared out the window, overwhelmed.

"What about the rock?" Gimble asked. "Will that help?"

Phoebe flipped through her notes. "I'm not sure. Nuummite has been around even longer than 'the mother of all poisons.' It's the oldest mineral on earth, formed three or four billion years ago in a volcano in Greenland." She shook her head. "I can't believe I didn't know anything about it until now."

"If we're dealing with the occult, the stone probably represents something," Mulder said. "Like strength or fertility."

Gimble raised an eyebrow.

"Fertility?" She pressed her lips together, trying not to laugh.

"I was throwing out words." Mulder raked his hands through his hair, and it left pieces sticking up all over.

"Nuummite is associated with elemental magic and protection."

"That's something." The fire ignited in Mulder again. "It could explain the bird and the arrows."

"I don't think so." Gimble propped his elbows on the table. "There's plenty of elemental magic in D and D, and none of it involves stabbing birds with arrows made of human bones."

Phoebe picked up one of the books in front of Gimble. "You didn't find any connection between birds and arrows?"

"Of course I did. People use arrows to hunt them," he said. "Other than that? No. But I found plenty of other stuff." Gimble ran his finger down the margin of his notes. "Magpies are part of the crow family. They love shiny objects, and they steal all kinds of things to build their nests. Magpies are also really smart, and they can mimic the calls of other birds."

"None of that sounds relevant," Phoebe said.

Gimble looked up from his notes. "That's because I'm not finished. There's a ton of superstition and folklore about magpies, but none of it meshes. So here goes. In Europe, magpies are considered bad omens, and, according to an old Scottish superstition, if you see a magpie hanging out solo, it's a sign someone is going to die. But in Korea, magpies mean someone is bringing you good news, and in China, they're a sign of good fortune."

"I doubt anyone would stab a bird with arrows if they thought the bird was a sign of good luck," Phoebe said.

"It gets better. Or worse, depending on how you look at it. Magpies are also associated with witchcraft, the devil, and occult knowledge. And—this is my favorite part—they can also transport souls into the spirit realm and bring back messages from hell." Gimble leaned back with his hands behind his head, reveling in the moment.

"Nice work, man." Mulder wasn't ready to let himself feel hopeful yet. But he also didn't feel as hopeless. They were back in the game. "An occult connection could explain the arrows."

"Then we're dealing with dark magic, not harmless hippie stuff, like astral projection," Gimble said. He took a couple of his D & D dice out of his pocket and rolled them on the table.

Phoebe frowned. But she wasn't angry. This frown was different—a smaller crease between her eyebrows and a faraway look.

"What's wrong?" Mulder asked. "You're making that face."

"Which face?" Now it looked more like the angry frown.

"The face that means you're concentrating."

"Oh." She relaxed. "I just can't figure out how the nuummite fits in. It's a protective stone people use to *combat* negative energy. Why would a killer use it in a ritual that involves murdering a child, and then leave it on the body of the victim?"

"Maybe the killer doesn't know what it is?" Gimble offered. "He could be confusing it with a different black mineral."

She shook her head. "It's too obscure. And they call it the

Magician's Stone. If the killer is involved with the occult, he would know about it."

Mulder dropped down in the chair. "People don't use it for anything else?"

"Just for new age practices," she said. "The protection stuff I mentioned."

He reached for the book in front of her and flipped it around so he could read it. "Auric shielding and shamanic journeying? We're going to need a translator to explain all this new age crap."

"Look at the chapter title. It's called 'Healing Arts,'" she pointed out.

Mulder glanced at the clock.

1:15.

One hundred and eight and a half hours, at the most—that was how much time Sarah Lowe had left if the coroner had calculated Billy Christian's time of death correctly. And he knew those estimates weren't always accurate. What if no one found Sarah before then? Would she spend the last few days of her life waiting for someone to save her?

"If we really want to figure out if the killer is involved in the occult, we need to talk to people who know about that stuff," Gimble said.

Phoebe groaned. "This isn't the kind of thing I want to discuss with your dungeon master."

"I'm not talking about my dungeon master. I mean the people

who know about herbs and crystals, and dead birds with sticks in them."

"What you *meant* to say was, people interested in new age practices." Phoebe neatly stacked the books she'd been reading and stood. "I saw some pay phones when we came in. I'm going to check the Yellow Pages for new age stores. I'll be back."

Gimble rolled the dice on the table while they waited. "In D and D there's a monster that looks like a puma with tentacles growing out of its shoulders." He watched the dice each time he rolled. "It's called a Displacer Beast, and taking it down is hard, because the Displacer projects an illusion of itself nearby. So you end up attacking the illusion. What if we're chasing the illusion instead of the real monster?"

Mulder wondered the same thing, minus the part about the Displacer Beast. "I guess there's no way to tell until we get more information. But either way, we know the cops aren't chasing the real monster. They don't even believe he exists."

Phoebe knocked on the glass wall of the study room, from where she stood on the other side. She waved a yellow scrap of paper in the air, as students in the library hallway squeezed past her. "There's a new age bookstore in Craiger, Maryland," she said the moment she walked in. "I called to make sure they were open today, and the woman who answered the phone said the store is about an hour and a half from here, near the Patuxent River." Phoebe gathered her notes and rushed toward the door. "Come on," she called over her shoulder.

As she walked out the door, Gimble watched, his eyes lingering too far south.

"Stop staring at her ass, or you can walk to Maryland," Mulder warned.

Gimble stole another look. "It's worth it."

CHAPTER 16

Bowie, Maryland
4:40 P.M.

"Are you sure the lady on the phone said the bookstore was in Craiger?" Gimble asked from the backseat of the car, studying the map he'd bought when they stopped for gas.

Mulder had been driving around Bowie, Maryland, for twenty minutes while Gimble navigated, which wasn't easy to do when the town they were looking for wasn't on the map.

Phoebe turned around in her seat and glared at Gimble. "Of course I am. It says it right here." She held up the strip of paper she'd torn out of the Yellow Pages. "And I wrote down the directions she gave me on the back."

Gimble rotated the map until it was upside down. "Yeah, well, I've never heard of a town that isn't on a road map."

"Maybe it's small," she said, refusing to give an inch.

"What did the woman say exactly?" Mulder asked.

Phoebe blew out a long breath. "That the store is on Route 320A—"

"We're *on* 320A," Gimble pointed out.

"I wasn't finished," she snapped. "On 320A near Powdermill Road."

"Hold on," Gimble said. "Powdermill Road is on here. Keep going straight and we should run right into it."

The two-lane road was empty, and within minutes, Mulder spotted a metal road sign. WELCOME TO CRAIGER, MARYLAND.

Gimble shook his head. "What kind of town isn't on a map?"

"A town we probably shouldn't be visiting," Mulder said.

"It's right there." Phoebe pointed at a peach-colored building on the corner. BEYOND BEYOND was hand-painted on the wood, in rainbow colors.

He turned into the gravel driveway and parked. He was the first person out of the car, and he peered through the front window. Long counters with glass cases beneath ran along the wall. One cash register was near the front, next to an arched doorway, with COFFEE BAR written above it in loopy script. The shelves along the walls displayed crystals, tarot cards, books, and candles.

"There's a coffee bar inside," Mulder said. "Who gets coffee at a bar?"

"Maybe it's a joke." Gimble hopped the curb and walked up to the window. He cupped his hands around his eyes with his nose an inch from the glass and looked inside. "This must be the right place. It's full of candles and hippie junk."

"I'm going in to check it out. I could use some caffeine." Phoebe opened the door, and a lopsided wind chime jingled.

"We might as well go in, too." Gimble shrugged and followed her, hanging back enough to check out her ass again.

The moment Mulder stepped inside, he was hit with the overwhelming scent of cinnamon, sickeningly sweet flowers, and patchouli. He coughed and fanned the air.

"It's our signature blend of essential oils," said a willowy woman with a mane of unruly blond curls framing her face. She breezed toward Mulder. "We call it Sacred Dream."

Gimble glanced up from where he stood at a shelf, already toying with a head massager. The moment he saw the curvy woman with the wild hair, he gave her ass his full attention. At least he wasn't looking at Phoebe's anymore.

"It's *interesting*," Mulder said, referring to the noxious odor.

"I haven't seen you in the shop before, and I never forget a face." The woman winked at Mulder. "Corinda Howell. Psychic, medium, and co-owner of this beautiful sanctuary."

"Nice to meet you." Mulder shoved his hands in his pockets, suddenly self-conscious. "Fox Mulder."

"What a powerful name." She smiled.

Gimble rushed over and flicked his hair out of his eyes. "Gimble."

Corinda raised an eyebrow. "That's one I've never heard before."

He cleared his throat. "It's a family name."

"And that's Phoebe." Mulder nodded in her direction, but she wasn't paying attention. Not to them, anyway.

Under the archway, Phoebe was talking to one of the tallest men Mulder had ever seen. He didn't look as old as their parents—maybe thirty? But the guy's dark hair and confident posture reminded him of a movie star from the 1950s. Phoebe stared up at him like she was hypnotized.

Even if Mulder and Phoebe weren't together, he wasn't okay with some random older guy hitting on her. He strode over to them, with Gimble on his heels. When he reached the archway, he slid his arm around Phoebe's waist and thrust his other hand at the tall asshole talking to her. "Mulder."

Phoebe looked at Mulder like he was insane.

The tall guy towered over him, and Mulder expected him to make a dominant tough-guy move. Instead the guy studied him with the gentle eyes of an old soul.

"Sunlight." The man's voice sounded smooth, like liquid silver.

"What about it?" Mulder asked.

"I'm *it*," the movie star said.

"Sunlight is his *name*," Phoebe said.

"That's even weirder than mine," Gimble said, joining the conversation. "Name's Gimble, by the way. Your parents really named you that?"

Sunlight smiled. "I named myself."

Gimble whacked the giant in the arm as if they were best friends. "Me too. So do you play Dungeons and Dragons? I bet you'd kick ass."

Sunlight gave him a strange look. "I'm not familiar with it." Then he turned back to Phoebe. "It was a pleasure meeting you, Phoebe. And if you change your mind, you know where to find me."

Mulder wanted to punch him in the smooth-talking mouth.

Sunlight joined Corinda, the psychic medium, near the door where they huddled in a private conversation.

"If you change your mind about what?" Mulder asked Phoebe now that the guy was gone.

She shoved him and stalked toward the coffee bar, where a line was already forming from a group of people coming out of the back room.

He slipped into line beside her. "Think they were having a séance back there to commune with Elvis?" She gave him a dirty look.

"What?" Mulder threw up his hands, playing innocent.

"You're going to play dumb after that show you just put on?" She crossed her arms and stared straight ahead.

"I was looking out for you." It was a lame excuse, but he couldn't help being a little raw after their awkward conversation this morning. "That guy was probably thirty years old."

"I doubt it." She shrugged and moved forward as the line progressed.

"Why are you so mad? Were you interested in him or something?" Now he definitely sounded jealous.

Phoebe whipped around to face him. "Sunlight does private sessions, and he leads a new age group called Psychic Emergence. He was *inviting* me to their meeting."

"Psychic Emergence?" Gimble strolled up to them. "That's a stupid name. That guy should just start playing D and D. He'd learn a few things."

"Maybe I could've gotten some information from him if you had kept your ego in check," she snapped at Mulder.

"My ego?"

"Umm . . . sorry to interrupt," said a Latino guy standing behind them. "But this is a peaceful space. You don't want to argue in here."

A skittish girl next to him nodded and whispered, "Sunlight wouldn't like it."

Mulder stared at them in disbelief.

Phoebe smiled at them. "We're sorry."

The girl behind the coffee counter waved at Mulder and his friends. "Can I get you something?"

Phoebe and Gimble ordered caffeinated drinks with goofy new age names while Mulder stood behind them and sulked. He was still pissed off about Sunlight, and now Phoebe was mad at him. But mostly, Mulder was angry with himself for blowing his chance with her.

If I ever had one.

Something caught his eye. A biker wearing a black leather jacket stood at the creamer station, at the end of the coffee bar. A dingy white patch with black Gothic lettering arced across the back of his jacket. The patch read THE ILLUMINATES OF THANATEROS.

Gimble noticed Mulder staring and craned his neck to see what he'd missed.

"Check out his jacket," Mulder said, keeping his voice low. "What do you think it means?"

Gimble shrugged. "No clue. Maybe he's in a band."

Phoebe came up behind them. "Why are you whispering?"

Mulder tilted his head in the biker's direction. "Ever heard of the Illuminates of Thanateros?"

"Nope," she said.

Gimble removed the lid of his drink and took a sip. "It sounds occultish."

Phoebe rolled her eyes. "Or Greek."

"A second ago you thought it was the name of a band," Mulder reminded him.

"I said *maybe*."

"While you two argue, I'm going over there to find out." Phoebe headed straight for the creamer station and slipped into the empty spot next to the biker.

"Does she go rogue like that all the time?" Gimble asked.

A smile tugged at the corners of Mulder's lips. "Pretty much."

They followed her but hung back a little.

"Excuse me," Phoebe said to the biker as she poured milk in her coffee. "I love your jacket. I've never heard of the Illuminates of Thanateros."

The biker took a sip of his drink. He was older than that slimeball, Sunlight, and he looked Phoebe in the eye instead of looking her up and down. "It's a group I belong to. We meet in one of the back rooms."

She acted interested. "What kind of group?"

"We practice chaos magick," he said, as if it were something completely normal. "Have you heard of it?"

"No," she admitted. "But it sounds cool."

A line was beginning to form behind Phoebe and the biker, so they moved off to the side. The biker noticed Mulder and Gimble lurking and waved them over. "You're all welcome to come to the meeting."

"Thanks. I'm Phoebe, by the way." Mulder and Gimble walked up beside her, and she added, "These are my friends."

"Mulder." He didn't wait for an introduction.

"Sam."

Gimble held up two fingers. "I'm Gimble."

Sam did a double take. "Like from D and D?"

"You play?" Gimble could barely contain his excitement. The guy had just made his day. "I mean, of course you play if you recognized my name."

Sam laughed. "I used to play all the time. I was a paladin. Level sixteen. Chaos evil."

Chaos evil? Was this guy serious?

Phoebe leaned closer to Mulder. "He's talking about his character's alignment in the game," she whispered, anticipating his question. "It determines the character's ethics and morality."

"Is that so?"

Phoebe put a hand on her hip. "I told you I knew how to play."

"I'm a bard. Level thirteen. Chaos neutral," Gimble was telling Sam, who seemed impressed.

"Chaos neutral, huh? Good choice. It makes you unpredictable."

A blonde in a white dress embroidered with colorful flowers popped her head out of the back room, where the previous meeting had been held. "Let's get started, Illuminates."

"Why don't you come to the meeting and see what you think?" Sam suggested. "If you like D and D, you might dig it."

Gimble glanced at Phoebe and Mulder, and they both nodded.

"If you're sure it's cool," Gimble said.

Sam motioned for them to come with him. "Everything about

our group is cool, and we're always interested in hanging out with open-minded people who are curious about chaos magick."

"That's us. Open-minded and curious," Mulder said, in an attempt to sound enthusiastic. But with his dry tone, it came off more like sarcasm.

Sam gave him a strange look and led them into the meeting room, which doubled as storage space. Chairs were arranged in rows across from stacks of cardboard shipping boxes.

Mulder noticed other rooms, including a yoga studio. "Why meet in a storage room when there are so many other rooms back here?" he whispered to Phoebe.

"No clue. Maybe they're all booked."

"Sit anywhere you like," Sam said, taking a seat at the end of the second row.

They slipped past him and claimed three seats together, leaving an empty seat between Sam and them.

Other people drifted into the room and sat down, while the blonde in the embroidered dress walked past them to the back of the room, juggling a banner and boxes of doughnuts. Mulder listened to the conversations taking place around him. He didn't expect anyone to start talking about dead birds, but he was hoping for something related to protective stones—not a debate between the women sitting in the front about which member of the Bee Gees was the hottest.

The blond woman returned to the front of the room.

"Welcome, everyone. For those of you who are new, my name is Rain Sky." She paused and smiled at the three newbies. "If you have any questions, don't hesitate to ask."

Rain Sky? Real original.

Mulder zoned out while the ten Illuminates recited a pledge. ". . . and through the power of belief and the balance between Chaos and Law, we will stretch the limits of what is possible."

He elbowed Gimble and whispered, "Didn't your dad say—?"

His friend nodded. "Chaos and Law are two sides of the same coin." He took a black triangular die out of his pocket and rolled it between his fingers. "Unfortunately, the Major read about the concept in *Stormbringer*, and now he talks about it all the time. Apparently, Law is important to the *aliens*."

Gimble accidentally dropped the die, and it fell on the floor and rolled under his chair.

Mulder bent down to pick it up and his gaze locked on the wall behind them, where Rain had hung the banner, and he froze.

The symbol in the middle of the banner . . . Mulder had seen it before.

CHAPTER 17

Mulder stared at the symbol—a circle with eight arrows radiating from the center. It looked exactly like the arrows sticking out of the magpie's body.

Phoebe nudged him, but he couldn't look away. He heard her gasp, and a moment later Gimble whispered, "Is that . . . ?"

Mulder nodded.

Gimble leaned over and signaled Sam. "That symbol on the back wall is cool. What is it?"

"Most people call it the chaos symbol," Sam said. "But in chaos magick, we call it the Symbol of Eight."

Mulder sucked in a sharp breath.

Eight days. That's how long the killer keeps the kids alive. And the kids are eight years old.

"Why eight?" Phoebe asked.

"It's an important number in chaos magick. The eight arrows in the Symbol of Eight—the chaos symbol—represent all the possible paths chaos can take. And all eight arrows are exactly the same length to remind us there isn't one 'right' path."

Gimble nodded. "So it's a chaos magick thing?"

"Eight has been a powerful number throughout history," Sam explained. "In ancient Egypt and ancient Greece, with significance in math, science, music, and art."

Gimble gave Sam a blank stare, as if he was racking his brain trying to figure out what this guy knew that he didn't. But the moment Sam mentioned math, Phoebe was way ahead of him.

"You mean because eight is a Fibonacci number? Or are you referring to the fact that, aside from one, eight is the only positive Fibonacci number that's a perfect cube?" she asked Sam. "Obviously, eight is also a perfect power, and people describe the infinity symbol as a sideways eight."

Sam's eyes bugged out. "Yeah, all that."

His response didn't impress Phoebe. She was done with him. She raised her hand, middle-school-style. "Rain? We don't know much about chaos magick. Any chance we can get a crash course?"

"Of course." Rain seemed thrilled to explain. "Chaos magick is a new system of magic. It's about harnessing the power of belief and using it as a tool."

The last part got Mulder's attention. "How do you do that exactly?" he asked.

"One way is through reaching an altered state of consciousness called gnosis," Rain said. "We've been discussing it at the last few meetings. It's a practice that involves focusing all your energy on a single thought or desire."

Mulder was good at that.

"By believing something is possible, you can make it happen," a girl with a feathered roach clip in her hair added.

"Hmm . . . okay." Gimble nodded at her, but his expression made clear that he had no clue what she was talking about.

"Did anyone practice gnosis at home?" Rain asked the rest of the group.

Several hands flew up. The Illuminates took turns sharing the altered states they had—or hadn't—reached, which involved lots of sitting on the floor and repeating stupid mantras to "manifest their desires."

This is total crap, Mulder thought. *Except for the chaos symbol. That means something.*

"If you haven't achieved gnosis, don't give up," Rain told everyone.

"It's not really happening for me. What if I can't find a way to get to that place?" asked a woman wearing a clear pointed crystal around her neck.

"Belief has power," Rain assured her. "You can't achieve gnosis unless you believe it's within your reach. Chaos magick requires us to abandon logic and the limitations society has imposed on us. The power comes from taking the leap—giving in to chaos and trusting that it will reveal itself to you."

"So power comes from believing?" Phoebe asked.

"Not *from* it," Sam said. "Belief *is* the power."

The rest of the long meeting dragged on. Mulder caught bits and pieces of the discussion about crap like mind-clearing techniques and creating an optimal environment for gnosis. Phoebe took notes and Gimble asked a question every ten minutes, as if he was actually thinking about joining up.

Mulder couldn't get past the chaos symbol.

The Symbol of Eight.

Why would the killer re-create that symbol with the magpie and the arrows? Did he practice chaos magick, too? Nothing the Illuminates had talked about sounded dark or evil. Were they holding back because of the newcomers?

When the meeting ended, the Illuminates headed for the doughnuts on a folding table. Gimble started to go for a snack, but Mulder stopped him. "Don't let Sam leave yet. See what else you can get out of him."

"I'm on it." Gimble still stopped to grab a doughnut before he caught up to the biker.

"So what did you think?" Sam asked, brushing powdered sugar off his jacket.

"Chaos magick seems pretty deep, you know?" Gimble said. "I'm interested in learning more about it."

"Tell Rain you want to sign up for the mailing list," Sam said. "We send out a zine every other month. It has lots of info for beginners."

"That sounds great," Phoebe said. "We'll all sign up."

Sam cupped his hands and shouted, "Rain? We've got three more people for the mailing list. That makes sixteen."

She waved her clipboard at him. "Just send them to me before they leave."

Mulder wasn't giving the Illuminates his name and address. Maybe he'd write down his dad's office address at the State Department.

Mulder cleared his throat. "So, Sam? I have a question."

"Shoot."

"I like the concept that belief is a tool. But what if the beliefs of the person practicing chaos magick are on the darker side of the spectrum?"

Sam frowned. "Chaos magick is about transcendence. We don't allow people like that in our organization."

Rain overheard them. "We kicked someone out a few months

ago because he was into that kind of thing. He was always talking about the Eternal Champion and the war between Chaos and Law."

Gimble perked up. "The Eternal Champion from Michael Moorcock's books?"

Were they talking about *Stormbringer*? Mulder was beginning to feel like he was the only person who hadn't heard of the book until the Major gave him a copy.

"Have you read them? They were part of the foundation for the idea behind what we do here," Rain explained.

"I just read *Stormbringer*," Mulder admitted.

"Then imagine how annoying it would be to listen to some guy talk about the Eternal Champion like he was a real person." Roach Clip Girl rolled her eyes. "A hero fighting to restore the balance between Chaos and Law. The guy thought all the stuff in the Moorcock books was real. What was his name again?" Roach Clip Girl snapped her fingers. "Burt? Merle? No, Earl something . . . It's on the tip of my tongue."

Mulder doubted it. The roach clip in her hair seemed like more than a fashion statement.

"What was his name, Rain? Look it up." Roach Clip Girl gestured at Rain's clipboard. "Anyway, this Earl guy was a total creep, and he was obsessed with Rain. He kept telling her about his critical role in restoring the balance. Why can't I remember his name? Was it Ray? He worked at a nursery that sold exotic plants, and he kept bringing her weird gifts. Didn't he give you a Venus flytrap?" The girl grabbed the clipboard out of Rain's hand and flipped through the pages, scanning the names.

Rain nodded. "Yeah. I pawned it off on Corinda."

"Earl Roy!" Roach Clip Girl blurted out. "That was his name!"

"Okay, everyone. It's time to clean up and clear out," Rain said, taking the clipboard from her.

Mulder kept his eyes glued to the clipboard, and he noticed the moment Rain set it on the table next to the doughnuts. She puttered around the room, stacking chairs and collecting trash.

"What can I do?" Phoebe asked.

Rain took a rubber band off her wrist and gathered her hair into a ponytail. "You can finish clearing off the table and throw the trash bag in the dumpster out back, while I take down the banner."

"No problem." Phoebe looked at Gimble and Mulder and tilted her head in Rain's direction. *Keep her busy*, she mouthed.

"Let me help," Gimble said, following Rain.

Mulder took a step toward the refreshment table, where Phoebe was tossing crumpled napkins in the trash. She noticed and shook her head, warning him to keep his distance. He wandered over to Gimble and Rain but kept his eye on Phoebe.

"Should I throw away the paper tablecloth, too?" Phoebe called out.

"Sure." Rain paused as if she was about to say something else, but Gimble hit her with a hailstorm of questions.

"So if I'm trying to get into a gnostic state, is it better to practice in my bedroom or the family room?"

Mulder watched Phoebe in his peripheral vision until she made her move. As she gathered up the paper tablecloth, she pretended not to notice Rain's clipboard, and she shoved it into the black trash bag along with the rest of the trash.

After she tied it up, Mulder joined Gimble in hammering Rain with questions, as Phoebe speed-walked to the back door. She slipped out just moments before Rain freed the last corner of the banner. Mulder and Gimble stalled by folding the banner incorrectly, but Rain had it refolded in under a minute. She did a quick check of the room, and tucked the banner in her bag.

"Wait. Where's my clipboard?" She looked around. "I think I left it on the table."

Hurry up, Phoebe.

"Are you sure?" Gimble asked. "Because I lose things all the time."

Rain headed for the back door. "Phoebe?"

As Rain reached for the push bar on the door, it opened, and Phoebe walked in holding the clipboard.

"This was in the trash," Phoebe said, handing it to Rain. "It must've been on the table when I tossed the doughnut box and the tablecloth. I'm really sorry."

"Don't apologize. Accidents happen." Rain wrote down the fake addresses they gave her for the mailing list. As they exited the storage room, they parted ways at the coffee bar, where Rain stopped to catch up with Sam.

"Did you get it?" Mulder asked Phoebe as they walked toward the front of the store.

"I'm not even going to answer that," she said.

On their way out, Phoebe paused to scan the bookshelves. But Mulder couldn't get out of there fast enough. He wanted to see the address. He hovered by the door, waiting.

Gimble picked up a handful of maroon octagonal gemstones from a bowl by the door. "These look cool."

"Those are raw rubies." Corinda walked up behind him, her wild curls falling down her back. "They have healing properties."

A familiar black stone sat on the table next to the bowl. "What's this one called?" Mulder asked, even though he already knew the answer.

"Nuummite," Cordina said. "It's the oldest mineral on earth. In magical circles, it's known as the Magician's Stone."

"What is it used for?"

"It has powerful protective qualities that can strengthen the auric shield."

"I've never heard of an auric shield," Mulder said.

"It's a barrier that protects our aura from all the negative energy out there in the world." Corinda picked up the black stone. "Nuummite is also used for self-examination and shamanic journeying, an altered state shamans reach that allows them to travel to other planes."

Yeah, right, Mulder thought.

Roach Clip Girl was on her way out and noticed them talking to the shop owner. "Hey, Corinda? Remember the guy who bought Rain the Venus flytrap?"

Corinda nodded. "And who bought up all my nuummite?"

"I forgot about that," Roach Clip Girl said. "He'd sit there during the meetings, rubbing a stone the whole time."

"Did he buy anything else?" Mulder asked.

"No. I never would've sold him anything in the store if I'd known he was practicing dark magic."

"Excuse me?" Phoebe waved from where she stood at the counter holding a few books, including a familiar green paperback. "I'd like to buy these books."

"Of course." Corinda breezed over to the cash register.

"Gimble, bring one of those stones over here. I'll get you one," said Phoebe like an indulgent mom.

Gimble put a stone down on the counter and saw *Stormbringer.* "Save your money. I've got fifty copies at home."

Phoebe ignored him and paid.

"Come again," Corinda called out as they left.

"Can I see the address?" Mulder asked the second they left the store.

Phoebe took a paper napkin out of her pocket and handed it to him. "You're welcome."

"Thanks," he mumbled.

She took the copy of *Stormbringer* out of the bag.

"Why did you buy it?" Gimble asked her. "The Major already gave you a copy."

She flipped it over and read the description. "I don't have that one on me, and if Earl Roy is obsessed with this series and the Eternal Champion stuff, I want to know more about it."

Mulder unlocked the car and slid into the passenger seat. His thoughts were all over the place, and he wasn't really listening. But he caught that last part.

"Phoebe is right," he said. "We need to know as much as possible about the Eternal Champion."

Because I think we're going to meet him.

CHAPTER 18

Route 320A, Craiger, Maryland
8:02 P.M.

Mulder barely said a word as Phoebe pulled out of the parking lot and drove north on Route 320A, toward the address on the napkin. He was in no condition to drive.

Gimble leaned between the front seats to talk to Phoebe. "Earl Roy lives near the Patuxent Wildlife Refuge, about ten miles north of here, which isn't great news."

"Why not?" Suddenly, Phoebe looked worried.

"According to the map, it's in the middle of the woods."

Mulder snapped to attention. "I don't care. We're going to his house. Now."

"We don't know if he's the guy," Phoebe said patiently.

"He was into dark chaos magick that made the Illuminates

uncomfortable, and the arrows in the dead bird looked exactly like the chaos symbol," Mulder said. "And when the 'creep' wasn't busy polishing his stockpile of nuummite, he worked at a nursery that sold exotic plants, where he could've picked up plenty of gardening tips to help him take care of all the monkshood he's probably growing in his backyard. But you don't think he's the guy?"

Phoebe ignored his tone. "I'm saying that we don't know for sure. Maybe the reason all the pieces seem to fit is because we *want* them to fit. What if we're wrong?"

"And what if we're not?" Mulder fired back.

"Then it's probably a bad idea to show up at a serial killer's house and ring the doorbell like we're selling cookies," Gimble tossed out offhandedly.

"We need to think this through and come up with a plan, Fox. And I need a burger," she added.

"There's no time to stop. A little girl's life is on the line," Mulder said, as if he were the only one who cared.

Phoebe stiffened. "You think I don't know that? Even if he's not the killer, they said he was a creep. So I'm not driving up to his house and winging it. How will that help Sarah Lowe?"

Mulder shoved the napkin with Earl Roy's address into his pocket and slumped against the seat. Part of him knew that Phoebe was right, but the other part of him wanted to save that little girl no matter what it cost him. It wasn't just a pathetic attempt to redeem himself. Unless he found his sister, redemption wasn't a possibility. And even if he did find her, he would never be able to give her back all the time she'd lost.

But I can try to keep the same thing from happening to this little girl.

"There's a diner a mile up ahead." Gimble pointed out a sign. "It's on the way to Earl Roy's place."

"Fine." Mulder stared out the window at nothing.

"Are you sure this is a restaurant?" Mulder asked.

From the outside, Charlotte's Diner looked more like a house. Whoever owned the place hadn't put much effort into maintaining it, unless the peeling beige paint, dark window trim, and mismatched wooden chairs out front were supposed to be selling points.

"You agreed to stop." Phoebe walked past him and stood next to the door with her arms crossed.

Gimble shrugged and followed her. "I'm hungry, too. I haven't eaten anything all day except a cherry pie and a doughnut."

The thought of choking down even a saltine made Mulder feel ill. His head was filled with images of terrified children with poison seeping into their skin and the hands of a faceless stranger carving arrows from human bones.

Mulder just wanted to go to the address written on the napkin in his pocket. He needed to know the truth, even if it tore him apart. The feeling of *not* knowing festered like an open wound.

"Fox? Are you coming?" Phoebe called out.

"Yeah."

Mulder took a deep breath and followed his friends inside. He wasn't expecting much, and Charlotte's Diner didn't disappoint. It was basic—one room with the kitchen through a doorway in the back. Red-and-white-checkered tablecloths covered tables, with wooden chairs tucked under them. Black-and-white photos of lumberjacks standing beside felled trees and old sawmills hung on the walls, the way family photos adorned people's living rooms.

The diner was almost empty, but the whole place smelled like apple pie. A definite plus as far as Gimble and Phoebe were concerned.

Mulder didn't care. He wanted to get in and out.

They settled at a table in the back, and Phoebe and Gimble didn't waste a lot of time reading the menu. When the waitress walked over, dressed in a powder-blue 1950s-style button-down shirt and matching skirt, Gimble ticked off his order in record speed. "Can I get a bacon cheeseburger with everything, onion rings, an order of chili fries, and a vanilla milk shake?"

"As long as you've got money to pay the bill, you can order whatever you'd like." She turned to Phoebe. "How about you, hon?"

"A cheeseburger with a side of fries, and coffee with cream and sugar."

"I'll just have an iced tea," Mulder said.

"All right, then." The waitress tapped her pen on the copy of *Stormbringer* Phoebe had put on the table. "You kids read this? My nephew read it. It's all about the devil, if you ask me." She glared at the book as she ripped off their ticket, slipped her pad back into the top pocket of her shirt, and tucked the pen behind her ear.

Phoebe flipped through pages of *Stormbringer*. "Now that I know Miss Fire and Brimstone over there disapproves, I really want to read it."

"Are you sure you don't want to eat anything?" Gimble asked Mulder.

"Don't bother." Phoebe didn't look up from the book. "Fox is stubborn. If he didn't order, he won't eat. Give me the highlights of this thing, Gimble. I'm not sure I can get through this whole book without frying my brain."

"It's what the Major is always babbling about. The Eternal Champion series is all about the relationship between Chaos and Law and maintaining a balance between them. They call it the Cosmic Balance. That's where the Eternal Champion comes in. If one side gets a leg up, an Eternal Champion is summoned to restore the balance."

"And that's Elric, the albino elf, right?" Phoebe continued to skim and flip pages.

Gimble sighed. "Elric isn't an elf."

"Right. He's the hero and a badass warrior who comes to save everyone," she said.

Mulder shook his head. "Nope. Elric is weak and sickly. He gets his power from Stormbringer."

"The sword?" Phoebe asked.

The waitress arrived with their food and mixed up their orders, giving each person the wrong plate. Phoebe stirred her coffee and waited for her to leave before swapping plates.

"Yeah." Gimble took a bite of his burger. "There are two swords—Stormbringer, an Agent of Chaos, and its brother sword, Mournblade, an Agent of Law. But they're not regular swords. Stormbringer and Mournblade are actually demons that take the form of swords, and they feed on souls."

"Where do they get the souls?" Phoebe popped a fry into her mouth.

"If the Eternal Champion—"

"This guy, Elric." She flashed the cover at Gimble.

"Right. In that book it's Elric." He stole a fry from Phoebe's plate. "So if Elric kills, or even cuts someone with Stormbringer, it's demon dinnertime. And when Stormbringer gets a soul, Elric gets a hit of strength."

Mulder took over. "But there's a catch. Since Stormbringer is a demon, it has a mind and will of its own, meaning Elric doesn't have complete control over the sword. Sometimes, it's the other way around."

"The sword controls him?" Phoebe nodded her approval. "That's a cool twist."

Gimble waved at Mulder to get him to stop talking. "Don't give away the end. It's the best part." He turned to Phoebe. "The swords can cause bloodlust in the Eternal Champion, and the only way to satiate it is by killing. Just skip to the end and read the last couple pages."

"Keep talking." She started skimming the end of the book.

Mulder and Gimble ignored her and waited while she read.

Phoebe's eyes went wide. "This is intense. Stormbringer turns on the Eternal Champion . . . and the sword kills him!"

Gimble nodded enthusiastically. "Yeah, it's the big finale to the series." He sipped his milk shake and looked down at the table. "I hope my mom had a chance to finish it. I don't know if she ever got to the end."

Phoebe sensed she was missing something. She looked at Mulder, but he shook his head. She took the cue and went back to her fries and her conversation with Gimble.

"I'll stick with *Star Trek*," she said. "If Earl Roy really *believes* this stuff, he's certifiable."

"But he probably doesn't think he's crazy." Mulder turned the idea over in his mind. "Beliefs have power, like the Illuminates were talking about in the meeting. If a person believes in something enough, that belief becomes a reality. Rain and the other girl at the meeting said Earl Roy talked about having an important role in restoring the balance between Chaos and Law, and he was obsessed with the Eternal Champion. Maybe Earl Roy thinks *he's* the Eternal Champion, the big hero who's going to save the world."

Gimble nodded. "It makes sense. All the adults he killed were breaking the law or doing shady things. Taking them out could be his way of tipping the scales in Law's favor."

Phoebe wasn't buying it. "If Earl Roy is going after bad people like some kind of a vigilante, why would he kill innocent kids?"

"He wouldn't," Gimble said. "Not if he's playing the hero."

"And if Earl Roy thinks he's the Eternal Champion, wouldn't he have a soul-eating sword like the one in the book?" she asked. "Why would he poison Billy Christian instead of using a sword to stab him?"

"We're missing something, but we don't have time to figure it out now," Mulder said under his breath. "Are you guys done yet? We can't waste any more time." He fished some money out of his pocket and left it on the table to cover the bill.

Phoebe nodded. "We need to call the police."

Mulder's expression clouded over. "Why?"

"Fox, if you're right about even fifty percent of this, we have to tell the police so they'll go to Earl Roy's house," she said.

"We *tried* that already. Twice." Mulder's voice rose. "There's no way they'll believe any of this. We have to go find him ourselves."

The waitress scowled at them, and Phoebe gave her a fake smile. Then she turned back to Mulder. "Find him *ourselves*? Are you listening to yourself? Because you're acting irrational. We're not in DC. The police here might take this seriously, but we won't know unless we try."

"Let's go." Mulder stood up. "There's a pay phone outside. I'll get change."

Phoebe went to the restroom while Mulder and Gimble walked over to the waitress. She was standing by the window to the kitchen, chatting with the cook.

"Excuse me?" Gimble asked her. "Do you have change for a dollar?"

"Sure." She counted the coins and handed them to Gimble.

"And can you tell me where this is?" Mulder handed her the napkin with Earl Roy's address written on it.

"What are you doing?" Gimble whispered.

Mulder ignored him.

"Are you sure you've got the right address?" the waitress asked. "This is in the middle of the wildlife refuge."

"It's right," Mulder said, hoping it was true.

The waitress finished giving him directions just as Phoebe came out of the restroom. Mulder shoved the napkin in his pocket. "Don't say anything," he warned Gimble. "I only asked for directions in case we end up needing them."

"Whatever. It's your funeral."

Phoebe and Gimble followed Mulder outside and across the gravel to the pay phone. He dialed 911 and angled the receiver so they could listen.

"Police, fire, or paramedics?" the 911 operator asked on the other end of the line.

"Can you connect me to the local police department?" Mulder asked. "I need to speak to a police officer."

"You shouldn't call 911 for that, sir." The operator sounded annoyed. "You can call the sheriff's office directly."

"I'm sorry, but I'm at a pay phone and I don't have any more change. Can you connect me this once?"

"Please hold."

After a few moments, someone picked up. "Anne Arundel County Sheriff's Department. Deputy Johannesen. How can I help you?"

Mulder closed his eyes. "I'm calling in a tip related to a kidnapping in Washington, DC. Sarah Lowe? She disappeared from her house four days ago. I know who took her. The man's name is Earl Roy."

"And you saw him take the child?" the deputy asked.

"No. But—"

"Did you see him with the child after the kidnapping?"

"No. I've never seen him before," Mulder admitted.

"Do you have any evidence?"

"No. But—"

"Give us a call when you do." The deputy hung up.

Mulder slammed the receiver into the cradle.

Phoebe touched his shoulder. "Fox?"

"I told you they wouldn't believe me," he snapped. "What if Sarah doesn't have time for that? It's been four days. If we're right, she only has four days left. But what if we're *wrong*? We don't know what he's doing to her. We can't leave her there."

Phoebe grabbed him by the shoulders. "You need to calm down."

"We can't leave her there." His voice cracked.

Phoebe took his face in her hands. "She's not Samantha. This won't bring your sister back."

Mulder tried to look away, but Phoebe wouldn't let go.

"I want to hear you say it," she said gently.

He shook his head.

"I need you to say it."

The words wouldn't come. He tried to slip out of her grasp, but he was trapped—cornered with no way out except through.

"I know she's not Samantha." His chest tightened.

Every word felt like a betrayal.

"She's not Samantha." Mulder raised his eyes to meet Phoebe's. "Because I can save her."

CHAPTER 19

Gimble was already in the backseat of the Gremlin and Mulder had one leg in the car when he noticed that Phoebe hadn't moved from the pay phone.

"What's wrong?" Mulder asked, standing behind the open car door.

"I'm not going." Phoebe's arms were crossed, and her tone had a finality to it that Mulder recognized. She was digging in her heels. If he didn't change her mind fast, there would be no changing it.

"Are you mad because I asked for directions?"

"It's not about the directions. I'm not escorting you on a suicide mission. If you're right about Earl Roy, then he has killed at least half a dozen people."

Mulder tilted his head to look at her. "Most girls would find that endearing."

Phoebe stormed over and stopped on the other side of the open car door in front of him. "Don't crack jokes. Not now. This is serious."

The jokes were strategic, a tactic to convince her that he had his emotions under control again—that he was thinking things through.

He raised his hands in surrender. "You win. No more jokes."

She rolled her eyes. "I swear you have sarcasm running through your veins instead of blood."

"How about a compromise?" he asked. "We'll drive out to Earl Roy's place and take a look around. Maybe we'll find something we can take to the sheriff's office to convince the deputy that I was telling the truth."

"And if we don't?"

"We come up with Plan B. But I can't do this without you, Phoebe."

She threw her arms up and sighed. "Fine. But only if you swear that you won't do anything impulsive."

Mulder leaned over the top of the car door and whispered in her ear, "Kissing you was impulsive. Are you saying I shouldn't have done that?" He didn't know why he chose that moment to ask. But fear had the opposite effect on him than it had on most people. Instead of making Mulder hesitant, it gave him courage. The courage he should've had before.

Phoebe's gaze locked on his. "Maybe you should try kissing me on purpose sometime, unless you don't want whatever this thing is between us to go anywhere." She brought her mouth so close to his ear that he could feel the heat of her breath on his neck. "If that's the case, just stick with the hit-and-run make-out sessions."

She turned away and circled around the front of the car and climbed into the passenger seat.

"Phoebe . . ." Mulder wasn't sure if she heard him. Following the trail of a psychopath didn't scare him half as much as the thought of losing someone else he loved—even if that someone looked like she wanted to kill him herself.

He got into the car and glanced in the rearview mirror. Gimble held the map up to the dome light.

"Did you figure out where we're going?" Mulder asked.

"Keep heading north on 320A until you hit River Road. Then take a left."

Within minutes, the porch lights of Charlotte's Diner disappeared behind them, and the road went from dark as hell to pitch-black. Mulder turned onto River Road, a narrow stretch of asphalt that didn't even have a dividing line painted down the middle.

Mulder leaned closer to the steering wheel, squinting. "I can barely see past the headlights."

"Maybe you should get glasses." Phoebe couldn't resist teasing him.

"If I had glasses, I'd look too distinguished and handsome. Women would pass out wherever I went."

Phoebe groaned.

"Are you sure we're going the right way?" she asked, staring out the passenger-side window with her face an inch from the glass. "I haven't seen a single house since we turned off 320A."

"I'm positive," Gimble assured her. "The waitress said there are only a few houses out here, and they're all on this side of the Patuxent River."

"Maybe we passed it." Phoebe didn't want to admit she was nervous. None of them did. Or they would have to acknowledge the kind of risk they were taking by driving out here.

Gimble checked the map again. "I don't—"

"Wait!" Phoebe shouted, startling the crap out of Mulder. "Did you see that?"

"Not unless I ran over it." He couldn't risk taking his eyes off the road.

"Back up," she said.

"What was it?" Gimble asked.

Phoebe shook her head. "I'm not sure, but it was *something*."

"Gimble, keep an eye out for headlights behind us." Mulder threw the car in reverse.

"We haven't seen a car in fifteen minutes," Gimble said. Then he caught a glimpse of Mulder's tense expression in the rearview mirror, and he turned around and pretended to play lookout.

Phoebe stared out the back window. "Hold on. Stop."

The moment the Gremlin stopped she jumped out, leaving the car door open. The extra illumination provided Mulder with enough light to see a dented mailbox nailed to a post. He got out and walked around to the passenger side of the car.

Mulder bent down next to Phoebe and studied it. Letters were scratched into the metal on the side. *ER* and another letter that looked like a *P*.

Earl Roy.

Gimble stuck his head out the window. "Well?"

Mulder swallowed hard. "This is his house."

The dirt driveway beside the mailbox snaked into the trees, not much more than tire tracks through the brush. If Mulder had been alone, he would've taken off and followed it. He stood at the spot where the shoulder of River Road and the tire-marked dirt met.

Mulder and Phoebe got back into the car. Everyone stayed quiet as he turned and drove down the dirt path. He clutched the wheel with his sweaty palms as branches scraped against the sides of the Gremlin.

"What if he sees the car?" Phoebe whispered, as if Earl Roy could hear her.

"Pull up over there on the left." Gimble pointed to a patch of grass off to the side of the driveway.

"There's a light up ahead," Phoebe said. "See it?"

"I want to take a closer look." Mulder parked, killed the head-lights, and opened the door to step out, but Phoebe caught his arm.

"Are you sure about this? We could leave and go get the cops right now."

Because they've been so helpful up until now? Mulder thought.

Going to the cops was the smartest and safest option for *him*, but what about for Sarah Lowe? What if she was in there right now and she was hurt? Mulder imagined getting closer to the house and hearing the little girl's screams. He couldn't fail her.

And he couldn't walk away if there was a chance that Earl Roy had information about Samantha.

"I just want to take a look. What if the place is abandoned? Or he doesn't live there anymore and we drag the cops all the way out here? And that's assuming they'll listen to us. We don't have a lot to go on. I've already lost credibility with one police depart-ment." Mulder got out and pulled the seat forward for Gimble to climb out.

"So we're really doing this?" he asked.

"If you want to wait here, it's okay," Mulder told him.

Gimble noticed Phoebe getting out and stood straighter. "I'm cool."

The three friends walked down the driveway together, fol-lowing the dim yellow light as a beacon. Within a few yards, the house came into view. The porch light exposed bits and pieces of the dilapidated building. It resembled a shack more than a house.

"It's dark inside, and there aren't any cars out front." Secretly, Mulder felt relieved. "He's probably not home. Stay here while I check it out."

"That wasn't the deal," Phoebe reminded him.

"Look." Mulder pointed at the darkened windows. "Nobody's here. I just want to see what's around back."

"This is a bad idea." Gimble glanced over his shoulder. "What if the guy comes home?"

"Whistle or something."

"Isn't that kind of obvious?" Gimble asked.

"Don't worry." Mulder turned around and walked toward the run-down house. He was wasting time. "I'll be back in three minutes."

"Fox—" Phoebe pleaded.

He cared about Phoebe more than anyone except his mom, but he couldn't walk away from this, not even long enough to hunt down the backwoods police station in Craiger.

He stayed close to the trees that bordered the driveway and the edge of the yard—if a dirt patch edged with brambles qualified as a yard. As he moved toward the house and his eyes adjusted to the darkness, disturbing details revealed its condition. The porch slanted dangerously to one side, and the wooden railings were long gone. The planks that formed the exterior walls were in various stages of rot. It was the kind of house that usually had a CONDEMNED sign nailed to the front door.

The brush was thicker along the side of the house, and Mulder's feet kept getting caught on tree roots and vines. When he finally reached the backyard, what little illumination the dim porch light had offered was gone. A sliver of moonlight cut through the trees, casting a pale glow on a pile of scrap metal like you'd find in a junkyard.

It was tall enough for Mulder to crouch behind, and it would offer him a clear view of the back door. He darted toward the scrap pile, hyperaware of how loud each step sounded. But inside, the house remained dark. He felt stupid for being scared of a run-down old house and creepy shrubbery.

Why was he letting Phoebe and Gimble's paranoia rub off on him?

It was a straight shot to the back steps. It couldn't hurt to take a peek through the window in the door. He probably wouldn't see anything except an empty house and a dead end. Mulder moved around to the front of the scrap pile, and something hard jabbed his rib. He looked over, and it took him a second to realize what had poked him—the handlebar of a child's bike.

A chill traveled up his spine. He squinted, examining the mound of metal. Metallic strips of plastic glinted in the moonlight. Streamers hanging from a different set of handlebars. He reached out and ran his hands over the metal. Vinyl seats not much bigger than his palm. Little tires. The curves of multiple sets of handlebars.

Dozens of tricycles and bikes—some old and rusty and others that looked brand-new—were haphazardly piled into a mountain of childhood memories.

Who did they belong to? Where are these kids now?

Billy Christian and Sarah Lowe hadn't been riding their bikes when they were taken. Had that bastard kidnapped other kids who weren't in the newspaper articles he'd found?

An image flashed through his mind. A chopper-style metallic blue tricycle with a white seat and matching white handlebars, and two steps in the back. Samantha had picked it out herself when she four years old. In the toy store, she'd walked past the pink tricycles and stopped in front of the flashy blue trike. "This one," she'd said. Mulder remembered feeling like he spent the whole summer with one foot on the back of that thing while Samantha yelled, "Push me, Fox!"

A sudden wave of rage hit Mulder. He wanted to pull down every single one of the bikes and hurl them at Earl Roy's decrepit house.

Mulder crossed the yard, walked up a few steps to the back door, and peered through the dirty window. He made out the shapes of the refrigerator and the oven, and, down the hall, the pale glow from the porch light seeping in. He tried the door without thinking about it. The latch clicked, and it swung open.

There are no coincidences.

It had become Mulder's mantra, and this cemented his belief.

Fate had led him here.

In his gut, he knew Samantha wasn't in this house. But Earl Roy might have answers to the questions that had haunted him for 1,952 days.

Was Samantha still alive? If she wasn't, what had happened to her?

It might be too late to save his sister, but if Sarah Lowe was inside—or information that might help the police find her— maybe he could save that eight-year-old little girl.

He stepped over the threshold.

Take it easy. You'll be long gone before he comes home.

Mulder took a deep breath and walked straight through the shotgun-style house to the front door. He wanted to let Gimble and Phoebe know why he was taking so long, even though she would kill him when she realized he'd gone inside.

I'll make it up to her. All of it.

The tiny, outdated kitchen was surprisingly neat. In the hall- way, black-and-white photos, in simple wooden frames, hung on the wall. The place seemed sort of normal until Mulder spotted an ornately carved gold sofa in the living room and six mismatched gold chairs in the dining room. The chairs were upholstered in velvet, each one in a different color, and they reminded him of the fancy furniture in his aunt's sitting room that no butt had ever dented. They looked out of place in a house owned by a grown man.

On a small table next to the front door, a single silver frame was proudly displayed.

Mulder switched on the light and opened the front door to lean out. He waved, and Phoebe and Gimble emerged from the trees. Mulder couldn't see Phoebe's face, but he knew she was pissed.

Their silhouettes moved in the darkness, as if they were walking toward the house. Mulder ducked back inside and picked up the silver frame on the table. A child smiled back at him. He stared at the image, his heart galloping in his chest.

Then he caught a flash in his peripheral vision, and things happened in rapid succession, like falling dominoes.

An arm slid around Mulder's neck and jerked him off his feet—

The silver frame slipped out of his hand and crashed to the floor—

Mulder gasped, but he couldn't get any air.

A boy stared up at him from behind the spiderweb of broken glass in the frame.

Billy Christian.

The arm around Mulder's neck tightened and dragged him out of the doorway. His vision blurred in and out of focus.

A boot kicked the door.

The last thing Mulder saw was the front door slamming shut.

CHAPTER 20

X had trudged through the mud in his brand-new boots, following Mulder and his high-strung friends. He had sucked it up because the kid was smart, and there was a 90 percent chance that he was right about Earl Roy, a chaos magick fanatic who had gotten himself kicked out of the Illuminates of something-or-other, a club for new age weirdos.

In a less-than-genius move, Mulder and his friends had parked a bright orange AMC Gremlin next to the dirt road that served as Earl Roy's driveway. Anyone coming down the road would see the automotive eyesore from ten yards away.

That was how X ended up slogging through the mud. He had to park off River Road and circle through the woods to catch up to the kids without being seen.

Only, he wasn't fast enough. By the time he reached the front of the run-down shack, Mulder's friends were standing in the driveway, out in the open. Granted, X was wearing a pair of prototype night-vision goggles, but even without them, two blond teenagers weren't hard to spot.

Where the hell was Fox Mulder?

A light switched on in the front room of the house, and X's career flashed before his eyes—and if Mulder kept tempting fate, it would be a short one.

Because he watched Mulder open the front door of the sad excuse for a house and wave at his friends. The idiot must have a hero complex of epic proportions. X pictured Earl Roy pulling up in his truck and seeing the teenager standing in his living room.

Can this assignment get any worse?

The moment the thought crystalized in X's mind, he regretted letting himself think it. Things could always get worse, and in X's experience, they always did.

As he started to turn away, a hulking figure appeared behind Mulder and threw an arm around the teen's neck. His friends froze in their tracks. They must have seen the guy grab Fox, too. What they couldn't have seen without X's night vision was so chilling that it made the hairs on his arms stand on end.

The man behind Fox looked like he was wearing a white mask, like a psycho in a horror movie.

Earl Roy turned to kick the front door with his boot, and X realized it wasn't a mask.

It was paint.

X was ready to bolt for the door and go after the kid. But he couldn't let Fox or his friends see him.

"Get in the damn car," he muttered to himself, waiting for the other two kids to react.

But the girl recovered from the shock first and dragged the short kid toward the car. "That's right," X said. "Go get the cops."

He watched the Gremlin start up and swerve toward the main road.

But the car turned left instead of right. X cursed under his breath. They were driving in the wrong direction.

Did it really matter? The nearest sheriff's office was thirty minutes away—maybe more—and that was if you were driving in the *right* direction.

The second the Gremlin pulled away, X mobilized. He had to get Bill Mulder's son out of that house without letting the kid get a look at him—a smart kid with a memory like Fox's would recognize X from the DC police station for sure, and that wasn't allowed.

He went in through the front door and did a quick scan of the living room before moving on to the kitchen. It looked neat and clean at first glance, but he'd been in a house like this before—nondescript and too generic. X had grown up in one of these homes. The secrets were all there if you knew where to look.

He opened the pantry, half expecting a body to fall out. Something moved, and X stumbled back. A black mass scurried toward him.

A rat king.

A writhing mass of rats—their tails knotted and twisted, transforming them into a monstrous creature.

Some people believed that rat kings were bad omens, a phenomenon so rare that only a few specimens existed in natural history museums. But X knew better. The specimens existed all right, but there was nothing natural about them. X was eleven, maybe twelve, when he read about them in a book he brought home from the school library. One night, the book went missing. He found it in the living room. His father was sitting in his stained armchair, drunk as usual, with the book in his hand. "You know this nonsense isn't real, don't you?"

X hadn't moved.

"In this book, they asked all kinds of fancy scientists, and none of them could explain it." His father laughed, a spray of spit showering X and the book. "Bet they didn't ask a janitor."

His father took a swig from the bottle in his hand. "Rats aren't smart, but they'll do anything to survive. You see this?" He pointed to the photo of a rat king specimen. Twenty rats, their tails tangled and intertwined in the center, with their heads facing outward. "If rats got twisted up like this in real life, you know what they'd do?" He took another swig. "They'd chew their own tails off to get themselves free."

He jabbed at the photo. "People did this. Tied the rats' tails together so they couldn't get loose. Nature doesn't create monsters. Only men do that."

X watched the black mass of rats scurry into the living room, the pieces of string and yarn that Earl Roy had used to tie the animals together trailing after them.

Now X knew he was dealing with a monster.

Earl Roy would be holed up in the basement. When X tried the door, it was locked from the inside. He had two choices—break it down and protect Fox Mulder, the directive from Cigarette Smoking Man, or follow organization protocol and protect his identity. He knew which option his boss would expect him to make.

But how could he leave the kid?

X took a deep breath and thought about the boy trapped downstairs with a monster. Then he thought about another kid—a boy who stood in the corner for hours until he dropped from exhaustion, while his father got piss-drunk and berated him. A boy who put himself through college and joined the organization. There were sacrifices he wasn't willing to make.

X made his choice.

He walked into the kitchen and found an ancient black rotary phone. He dialed the number everyone knew by heart.

Then he turned around and walked out the back door.

CHAPTER 21

"Law chooses the sinners." The voice sounded loud and faraway at the same time.

Mulder's head felt heavy.

Was he dreaming?

No. That wasn't right. . . .

Mulder sucked in a deep breath. What was that smell? Perfume? Flowers? He tried to stretch, but he couldn't move his arms.

Something was wrong.

Another sound permeated the fog clouding his thoughts—a warbling chatter. "Sing for me, and I'll give you more steak," said a man with a gravelly voice. It was the same voice Mulder had just heard. He forced his eyes open and immediately regretted it. The soft light in the room blinded him, as if he were staring at the sun. Mulder tried to shield his eyes, but he couldn't bring his arms up in front of him. It took a second for it to register that his wrists were bound behind his back, and he was staring at thin metal bars.

Then he remembered—walking through Earl Roy's house and turning on the light, Phoebe and Gimble coming toward him, feeling an arm around his throat, and Billy Christian's face behind broken glass.

Mulder was in some kind of a metal cage. If he slouched, he could sit up without bumping his head. He bent down to read a ripped silver sticker near the bottom of the cage: HAPPY DOG HOUSES.

He was in a dog kennel.

Realization set in—along with panic. The man who had choked him out and locked him in there had already murdered one child and kidnapped another. What would he do to Mulder, an intruder who'd broken into his house?

Kill me.

He couldn't afford to think that way. Gimble and Phoebe must have seen Earl Roy grab him, so the police were probably already on their way.

I'm going to make it out of here, and Sarah will, too.

Mulder surveyed his surroundings. The combination of the rough stone walls and thick pillar candles bathing the room in yellow light, the place looked like a cross between a medieval castle and the headquarters of a secret society.

The chaos symbol, or the Symbol of Eight as the Illuminates called it, was hand-painted on the wall in black paint that had dripped in places, leaving long streaks running down to the floor. The opposite wall was covered with writing and a single arrow pointing straight up, and white rose petals littered the smooth stone floor.

Across the room, a fancy gilded birdcage hung from the ceiling with a black-and-white bird inside that alternated between chattering and the warbling call he'd heard a minute ago. It looked exactly like the magpie Mulder had seen lying on Billy Christian's chest in the cemetery.

Earl Roy was nowhere in sight.

Muffled sounds echoed from the other side of the wall—footsteps, a bell ringing, scraping, and the same gravelly voice, muttering and singing. Mulder maneuvered back down onto his side to make it appear as if he were still unconscious. The angle allowed him to peek up from the bottom of the cage and keep watch.

A broad-shouldered man backed into the room, dragging something. The soles of his heavy work boots thudded against the stone floor, each step slow and deliberate. The top half of his blue coveralls hung around his waist, and the back of his white undershirt was stained with sweat. He was holding the top of a fancy gold chair like the ones upstairs, tilting it back carefully as he pulled it into the room.

Earl Roy had something white all over his arms and hands. It wasn't chalky like baby powder. It looked more like house paint. But the man had his back to Mulder, so he couldn't see much without sitting up. The magpie chattered, and Earl Roy lowered the front legs of the chair and left it facing the wall.

He turned and pointed at the cage. "Don't test me."

Mulder saw Earl Roy's face and froze. A pair of blue eyes stared out from a mask of white that covered every inch of the man's face and blended into his hairline and down his neck in sloppy strokes. The opaque color and greasy texture reminded Mulder of the makeup clowns and mimes used to paint their faces.

Or the cover of *Stormbringer.*

An albino warrior.

Earl Roy had transformed himself into the image of the Eternal Champion, Elric from the book. The effect erased the killer's features, except for the panicked blue eyes darting around the room.

"Four more days," Earl Roy said to himself, using the hushed tone of someone keeping a secret—or trying to talk himself out of doing something rash. "You can wait four more days to destroy the demon. You've done it before."

Four more days.

He was talking about day eight, when he killed the kids.

Mulder's logical side told him to stay quiet and hope that Earl Roy left the room long enough for Mulder to work his hands free. But logic almost never won out with him. He acted on instinct. Right now, his gut was telling him to get as much information about Earl Roy as possible.

Initiating a conversation with an unstable man seemed risky, but he wasn't about to sit in a dog kennel and do nothing.

"What happens in four days?" Mulder asked, his voice not much louder than a whisper.

"The cycle will begin again." Earl Roy didn't look at him, but at least he didn't seem irritated that Mulder had spoken to him.

Mulder scooted to the side of the cage that was closer to Earl Roy, and he saw something dangling from the seat of the chair.

Two small feet.

"Leave me alone. It's not your decision," Earl Roy said, facing the birdcage and the back of the chair. Was he talking to the bird again? He turned the chair around, leaving streaks of white greasepaint on the blue velvet.

Sarah Lowe was propped up in the gold chair, her small body nestled against velvet. She was dressed in a white gown, with her blond hair neatly brushed and a garland of white roses draped over her shoulders like a mantle. The top of the chair was decorated with silver Christmas tinsel and cheap gift-wrap bows like a makeshift throne. Strips of fabric were wrapped around her chest and wrists and tied in loopy bows, securing her to the chair.

The child's eyes were shut, but Mulder saw her shoulders quiver as if she was having a bad dream. She looked drugged, most likely with a sedative like the one listed on Billy Christian's autopsy report.

"The vessel is making an honorable sacrifice. You want a gift?" Earl Roy stood in front of Sarah, looking disgusted. "In four days, I'll give you the gift you deserve."

What the hell is going on?

Earl Roy stormed out of the room. Mulder heard the bell again and more shuffling. He caught a glimpse of something pink near the doorway.

No . . .

Mulder tasted bile in the back of his throat. Earl Roy was pushing a child-sized pink bicycle with rainbow-colored streamers and a shiny gold bell. Mulder's mind flashed back to the scrap pile of bikes behind the house. Had those been "gifts" for other children once?

"Here it is," Earl Roy said proudly as he presented the bike to the drugged child.

Play along. Get him talking again.

Mulder cleared his throat. "That's a really nice bike," he said, fighting to stay calm. "Are you going to let her ride it?"

"I never had a bike." The killer turned toward Mulder, but he didn't make eye contact. "My father said bikes were expensive. Special things for special people." He wandered over to the pink bicycle and rang the gold bell. "He said I wasn't special enough to have one." His painted white lips formed a hard line, and he shook his head. "Me. The only human who can see the sword."

Mulder had Earl Roy talking. But now that he did, how was he supposed to respond? He needed the Major to translate.

"If you let the drugs wear off, Sarah can ride the bike when she wakes up," Mulder said. "You didn't give her anything that will hurt her, did you?"

Earl Roy gestured at the little girl, confused by the question. "Stormbringer doesn't need protection."

Why is he calling her Stormbringer?

In the books, Stormbringer was a demon that took the form of a sword—not a child.

Was Earl Roy hallucinating? He was definitely delusional. But he believed every word he was saying.

And there is power in belief.

"But the little girl in that chair isn't a sword," Mulder said.

The killer approached the cage, his white face inches from the thin metal bars. He curled his fingers around them. "*You* can't see the blade glowing inside her. I'm the only one who can, because *I am* special." He peeked over his shoulder again, as if he thought Sarah—or in his mind, the demon-sword, Stormbringer—was eavesdropping on their conversation. "In this world, the children are the vessels. That's how Stormbringer torments me. It knows I don't want to hurt innocents."

Mulder thought about the end of the novel. The demon-sword turned on the Eternal Champion and killed him. Was Earl Roy afraid the same thing would happen to him?

"Is that the reason you kill the kids?" he asked. "To keep Stormbringer from hurting you?"

"The demon won't hurt me. I feed it souls. It's the Eternal Champion it wants." Earl Roy wasn't making sense.

Wasn't he supposed to be the Eternal Champion?

But Earl Roy kept talking about the Eternal Champion like he was another person. Was the Champion a hallucination, like the glowing swords he saw inside the children? Or a voice in his head?

The magpie chattered, and Earl Roy glared at Sarah. "Don't whisper your lies to the bird. It obeys the Eternal Champion, and it will transport the child's soul to the next life, where it can find peace." The lunatic was getting more agitated by the second. "Then I will bury the vessel's body in a place of honor."

Earl Roy pounded his fists against his temples—over and over. "Stay out of my head, Stormbringer, or I'll sing the song. 'As Chaos lays me down to sleep, I beg the Law my soul to keep. . . .'"

"Is that why you killed the adults? The 'sinners' whose bones you took? Like the slumlord and the psychiatrist? Did you kill them so you could feed Stormbringer their souls? I would understand if you did," Mulder lied. "The demon told you to do it, right? And they were bad people anyway."

"True. But that's not my job, and I could never do it anyway."

"Then who killed them?" Mulder asked.

"Law chooses the sinners." Earl Roy tilted his head and gave Mulder a curious look. "The next person he picks could be anyone. Even you."

Mulder pictured the Major's map. He kept coming back to the distance between this house and the locations where the adult murder victims were discovered. Some of the crime scene locations, like the waterfront in DC, were a trek. Would a serial killer leave the kids alone for that long?

Mulder's gut feeling kicked in, and he realized there was another possibility. . . .

Maybe we've had this all wrong.

He searched the killer's empty eyes. "Are you the Eternal Champion?"

Earl Roy shook his head. "No."

"But you kept talking about the Eternal Champion . . . and you have Stormbringer, his sword." Mulder sounded crazy, but he couldn't stop himself. "What about your skin? You painted it white like Elric's. Why would you do that if you're not the Eternal Champion?"

"Because I'm his protector."

CHAPTER 22

Mulder remembered that detail from the novel. "Right. The Eternal Champion always has a companion—a protector."

"It's my job to destroy Stormbringer before the demon becomes too powerful to control. The sword can't be trusted. It will betray the Eternal Champion and kill him. But I figured out how to change the story."

"How?" Mulder coaxed.

"The Eternal Champion never wields Stormbringer. The sword and the vessel stay with me." Earl Roy dragged a hand over his face, smearing white paint down his cheek. "Until midnight on the eighth day, when I destroy it. But Stormbringer always comes back. It finds another vessel, and the Eternal Champion makes me retrieve it."

"In the books, the Eternal Champion gets power from Storm-bringer in exchange for feeding the sword souls," Mulder pointed out. "If Stormbringer stays with you, then how does the Eternal Champion get the power he needs to restore the balance between Chaos and Law?"

"The Eternal Champion gives me the bones of the sinners, and I deliver them to Stormbringer."

"But that's not how it works in the books," Mulder argued. "You can't just rewrite the story. It's already been written."

"Shut up!" Earl Roy whipped around as if someone had called his name, rage flashing in his eyes. "You don't know anything about the way things work. You shouldn't even be here. Whatever happens isn't my fault." He walked over to the creepy throne and stopped in front of Sarah. He nodded as if she were speaking to him. "If I do it, you have to leave me alone. Just for a little while," Earl Roy pleaded.

Mulder's stomach bottomed out. A deranged serial killer was bargaining with the psychotic voice in his head, and from what Mulder could tell, his soul was the bargaining chip.

Earl Roy slid on a pair of yellow rubber gloves and picked up a wide paintbrush like the kind Mulder's mom used to paint their kitchen, and a glass container. He opened the container carefully and scooped out a brush full of brownish green pulp.

Aconite. The poison that killed Billy Christian.

Earl Roy must have mashed up the leaves.

"'As Chaos lays me down to sleep, I beg the Law my soul to keep. . . .'"

"What are you doing?" Mulder squeezed himself into the back corner of the cage and desperately felt around for a rough piece of metal he could saw the ropes against. Logic told him he'd never have time to cut through even an inch, but it was a Hail Mary.

"It's not my fault," Earl Roy said as he walked toward the cage. "Stormbringer wants a soul. You weren't supposed to be here."

Mulder looked over at the little girl as he worked the ropes against the cage. He had failed again. Maybe Phoebe and Gimble would make it back here in time to save her.

Earl Roy bent down in front of the cage and unlocked it with one hand, holding the paintbrush in his other hand.

This is it.

If Mulder was going to die tonight, he wanted to die with an answer to the question that had never stopped haunting him.

"Did Samantha Mulder sacrifice herself, too? November 27, 1973. Chilmark, Massachusetts, 2790 Vine Street. Did you kidnap her?" he shouted.

"'When in the dark of night I wake, show me the soul that I must take.'" Earl Roy reached inside the cage.

Mulder kicked, but the killer grabbed his leg and dragged him out on his back. Mulder's hand scraped against a piece of rough metal, and his head hit the lip of the cage, then slammed against the stone floor.

Earl Roy froze and pointed a shaky finger at Mulder. "What's on your hand?"

Is he talking to me?

"Is that . . . ?" Earl Roy's eyes went wild. He let go of Mulder's leg and scrambled backward, gagging and dry-heaving. Tossing the paintbrush aside, he struggled to peel off the yellow gloves. His eyes darted to the floor next to Mulder, and he gagged again, shielding his eyes with his arm.

Mulder looked around.

A red streak of blood was smeared on the floor.

He sat up and twisted so he could see his hands. One of them was bleeding. He must have cut it on the cage, but it was no big deal. At least not to him.

But Earl Roy was acting like Mulder had severed a limb. "Don't look," he tried to comfort himself.

Mulder turned so his bloody palm was facing Earl Roy. "At my hand? It will stop bleeding. I hope," he added, using the kidnapper's phobia against him.

"Clean it up. All of it." Earl Roy kept his face shielded.

"I don't know if I can," Mulder said. "There's sooo much blood."

Earl Roy made the mistake of moving his arm and caught sight of the blood. He gagged again, and this time he puked down the front of his undershirt.

The truth hit Mulder so hard that he felt sick, too.

The killer who had mutilated the bodies of his adult victims to remove their bones wouldn't throw up at the sight of blood.

The man cowering in front of him wasn't capable of executing either of those tasks.

Which means there's a second killer. The real Eternal Champion.

Earl Roy wiped his mouth on his sleeve and staggered out of the room. Mulder got on his knees and crawled toward the pair of yellow rubber gloves on the floor. He wanted to get to the paintbrush, but with his hands bound, he probably couldn't slip the gloves on to pick it up. He still had to try. Even if he couldn't stop Earl Roy, slowing the guy down was the next best thing.

But Mulder didn't get anywhere near the gloves or the paintbrush, because Earl Roy returned a minute later carrying a heavy moving blanket and a stack of rags. He had something else in his other hand, but Mulder couldn't see it.

Earl Roy opened one eye just enough to determine Mulder's location and tossed the rags at him. "Clean it up now!" he roared. "All of it!"

"And if I don't?" Mulder challenged him.

The killer bolted across the room and picked up the pink bike. He hurled it straight at Mulder. The bike missed him by inches, and it crashed into the cage.

"If you don't, I will throw this blanket over you and beat you until you lose consciousness again." Rage flashed in Earl Roy's eyes. "Then I'll deal with Stormbringer." He raised his other hand and Mulder finally saw what he was holding.

A baseball bat.

Fear ripped through him, destroying his false sense of calm. "You don't want to hit me with that. I'll bleed even more."

"That all depends on where I hit you." Earl Roy dropped the blanket and kicked it across the floor. "Get under the blanket."

"Wait. Just listen," Mulder pleaded.

"I'm done listening to you and the sword."

"Just give me a second."

"Get under the blanket now!" he shouted.

"I'm doing it." Mulder crawled under as Earl Roy closed in on him.

Then Mulder heard a sound—

Pounding.

Followed by stairs creaking and voices.

An army's worth of black boots came down the steps.

"County sheriff. Put your hands in the air," an officer shouted at Earl Roy.

"Don't touch the paintbrush on the floor," Mulder warned. "It has poison all over it."

When the deputies realized Earl Roy wasn't armed, three of them rushed the killer and threw him to the ground, while another cop grabbed Mulder by the shoulders and dragged him out of the way.

"There's a little girl over there." Mulder nodded in Sarah's direction. "I think she was drugged. Her name is Sarah Lowe. Please help her."

Another officer rushed to the child's side.

The cop quickly untied the rope around Mulder's wrists. "Are you all right?"

Mulder nodded.

Not even close.

Earl Roy was lying on his stomach, with his hands cuffed behind his back. Most of the white paint had smeared off his face, and he looked more like a regular person.

Monsters shouldn't be able to blend in with normal people. If a kid came face-to-face with one, how were they supposed to know?

A deputy freed Sarah Lowe and wrapped his jacket around her small frame to scoop her up into his arms. Mulder rushed over and wrapped the edges of the jacket tighter around the little girl.

"Will she be okay?" He swallowed hard, afraid of the answer.

"I don't know what he gave her, but an ambulance is on its way." The deputy noticed the worried look in Mulder's eyes and added, "But she's breathing and her pulse rate is normal, and those are good signs."

The sheriff surveyed the symbols painted on the walls with a look of pure disgust and stormed over to the spot where the killer was lying on the floor.

"Earl Roy Propps, you're under arrest." The sheriff nodded at one of his deputies. "Read the son of a bitch his rights."

Earl Roy began to sing. "'As Chaos lays me down to sleep, I beg the Law my soul to keep. . . .'"

"What are you waiting for? Get those kids out of here." The sheriff motioned to the stairs, then returned to issuing orders to the rest of his team. The deputy carried Sarah as he led Mulder along the perimeter of the room to the stairs.

The sheriff caught up with them on the first floor. "I'll need to take your statement. But I'm curious. How did you end up here tonight?"

"Didn't my friends tell you?" Knowing Phoebe, she probably hadn't wasted any time on the details.

"You mean those kids outside in the orange car?"

"Yeah."

"We haven't talked to them yet," the sheriff said. "Someone called in an anonymous tip. The caller said he witnessed a man dragging an unconscious teenager into a house and gave us this address."

An anonymous tip?

This house was in the middle of a wildlife refuge, and nobody except Mulder's friends had been around when Earl Roy choked him out. Why would Phoebe and Gimble call in a tip instead of just telling the cops what happened?

When they reached the front door, Mulder stopped. "Sheriff, there's something I need to tell you."

"What's on your mind?"

Mulder rubbed the back of his head, where a huge knot had formed. "Earl Roy wasn't working alone. He has a partner, and the other killer is still out there."

The sheriff put his hand on Mulder's shoulder. "You've had a rough night, and I think you're in shock. It can cause paranoia. But it's normal. It'll pass."

"I'm not in shock. Earl Roy can't stand the sight of blood. He's terrified of it. I cut my hand and—"

"You need some rest, son."

"I'm fine. I swear. If you could just—"

The deputy nudged open the front door, and when the paramedics saw the child in his arms, they descended on Sarah Lowe and whisked her away. The dirt driveway was now a sea of police cars and flashing lights.

"Fox?" Phoebe shouted, racing up the porch steps. Her pigtails had come loose and her hair was tangled. She threw her arms around him and squeezed. "I'm sorry. We tried to find the police station."

"But we went the wrong way," Gimble said apologetically.

"The sheriff said someone called in an anonymous tip. Why didn't you just tell them who you were?" Mulder asked.

Phoebe looked confused. "It wasn't us. I turned the wrong way on the main road. Eventually, we figured it out and turned around. Then we saw the police cars, so I followed them."

"Then who called in the tip?" Mulder was stumped. The hair on the back of his next stood on end. Had someone else been watching them?

Gimble shrugged. "I don't know. Just be happy they did."

A paramedic slipped past Gimble and Phoebe and approached Mulder. "I need to check you out."

"I'm okay."

"Let's make sure." The paramedic examined Mulder's hand.

"Is the little girl all right?" Mulder asked.

He nodded. "She's still disoriented, but her vital signs are good."

"You saved her life." Phoebe rested her head on Mulder's shoulder and reached for his hand. She noticed the blood and gasped. "You're hurt!"

"It's no big deal." Mulder smiled as Phoebe studied his palm with the intensity of a surgeon. Secretly, he loved having her fussing over him.

The paramedic swabbed the cut with some antiseptic and wrapped a bandage around it. Then he asked Mulder some questions and shined a light in his eyes to check for a concussion. "Everything looks good, but you should still go to the ER and let a doctor examine you. And get a tetanus shot for the cut. A deputy found a bunch of rats in the kitchen."

"Okay," Mulder said, although he had no intention of going to the ER. He wanted to get as far away from this house as possible.

The sheriff asked Mulder some questions, and he recounted his story while Phoebe bit her nails and Gimble paced.

"If I hadn't seen that basement for myself, I'm not sure I would've believed it." The sheriff handed him a business card. "Give me a call if you remember anything else."

"Let's get out of here." Phoebe took Mulder's uncut hand, interlacing her fingers with his. "I'm sure I'll have nightmares about this place."

"Yeah. Me too."

Phoebe squeezed his hand and leaned closer. "You don't really sleep anyway."

"I did when you were in my bed," he whispered. "Maybe you need to be in it more often." Mulder wasn't actually flirting. He meant it. His emotions were too raw right now to joke about anything.

Phoebe's blue eyes searched Mulder's brown ones, and her eyes welled.

"What's wrong?" He wrapped his arm around her back, their fingers still interlaced, and pulled Phoebe against his chest.

She shook her head. "I'm going to sound heartless for saying this after you just saved a kid's life. . . ." She took a shaky breath.

Mulder watched her long lashes brush her flushed cheeks. One day he'd work up the nerve to tell Phoebe how he really felt about her.

"Come on, tell me."

"Don't do anything like that again, Fox. Please. I need you to start caring about yourself. Because I care about you . . . a lot."

"How much is a lot?" He flashed her a sheepish smile.

She gave him a little shove. "You know what I mean."

Mulder pulled her toward him. When their lips met, the kiss didn't feel like any of their previous kisses.

This kiss burned its way through his body, right down to his soul. It was made of fear and heartache, relief and anticipation, promises and hopes. It reminded him that he still had someone to hold on to in this screwed-up world.

Mulder and Phoebe clung to each other, kissing in the darkness, and for a few minutes, his life was perfect.

CHAPTER 23

Washington, D.C.
April 3, 2:00 A.M.

Mulder had mentally rehearsed the story he planned to tell his father on the ride back from Craiger to DC. He was done lying and holding back to make his parents happy.

Maybe *happy* was the wrong word.

Nothing made his mom and dad happy. Nothing had since the night his sister vanished. Mulder was just something that Samantha's kidnapper had left behind, like a smudged fingerprint—proof that the kidnapper had been there, without leaving anyone a trail to follow.

When he finally made it home, all that rehearsing in the car turned out to be a waste, because his father wasn't there. Phoebe curled up on the sofa while Mulder took the longest shower of his life. He scrubbed his skin until it burned. Being in the same room with a monster who killed kids had left a permanent stain on him, like a different kind of poison.

He toweled off and slid on his last clean pair of jeans. The clothes he had been wearing earlier lay in a heap on the bathroom floor. Mulder picked them up and stuffed them in the trash can, then washed his hands, twice.

In the living room, Phoebe was asleep on the sofa. Mulder thought about waking her up, but she was out cold. He unfolded an afghan from the chair and draped it over her. For a few minutes, he just watched her.

What if Earl Roy had been outside his run-down house earlier tonight, and he had grabbed Phoebe instead of him? He never should've put her, or Gimble, at risk.

I should stick to screwing up my own life.

With Phoebe on the sofa, Mulder had no choice but to sleep in his room—meaning lie awake all night in there. He walked down the hallway and stopped in front of his bedroom door. He put his hand on the knob and closed his eyes. It was the same thing he did whenever he stood on this side of the door alone.

Mulder kept his squeezed eyes shut until he entered the room. He imagined opening them and seeing Samantha sitting on his bed, mixing up his basketball cards, as if she had never left. As a kid, he had believed that if he kept doing it, one day he would open his eyes and Samantha would be there. His heart thudded in his chest, and he slowly opened his eyes.

Like all the other times, Samantha wasn't sitting on the bed.

The room was empty.

The Illuminates of Thanateros were wrong. Believing in something enough couldn't make it happen, at least not for him.

Mulder spent most of the night rereading chapters from psychology textbooks, serial killer autobiographies, and John Brophy's *The Meaning of Murder*. He sat on the floor with his back against the wall, surrounded by books about killers, and for the first time in months, he fell asleep before the sun rose.

Mulder woke up the next morning to the sound of the phone ringing. He jumped to his feet and bolted to the phone in his dad's room. If it was his mom, he didn't want her to worry.

"Hello?" he said, out of breath.

"It's your father." Mulder's dad always felt the need to get that out, as if he was worried Mulder might forget.

"Where are you? I thought you were coming home last night?"

His dad sighed, and Mulder knew what was coming next. "I'm still in New Mexico. I need to stay here for three more days. Some unexpected things happened, and now I can't leave. The Project is at a critical stage."

Some unexpected things happened here, too.

Mulder heard his dad cover the receiver and talk to someone in the room with him. ". . . timeline changed . . . results . . . the merchandise . . . okay . . . tell Openshaw I'm on my way." Then his dad came back on the line. "Mulder, did you hear me?"

"Loud and clear," he said, feeling strangely immune to the disappointment. He wasn't going to bother telling his dad about what had happened. He could find out when he got home.

"I'll call you tonight." His father didn't even mention Phoebe or remind him to sleep on the sofa, which meant he'd forgotten she was visiting.

"Okay." Mulder hung up. He wouldn't call, and they both knew it.

The weird part?

He didn't care anymore. Mulder was more interested in talking to Gimble's father than to his own.

After witnessing Earl Roy's reaction last night when Mulder cut himself, it was obvious the man couldn't have hacked up anyone to steal their bones. And his delusion wasn't what they had originally thought. There was another serial killer walking the streets.

But how was Mulder supposed to find him? The killer must

have left behind a clue that he'd missed, and nobody knew more about the Eternal Champion or the adult victims than the Major.

Mulder called Gimble, hoping the phone was plugged in. After the third ring, he was about to give up.

"Hello?" Gimble asked hesitantly.

"It's me. I need to come over and talk to your dad."

"Are you doing okay? I'm still pretty freaked out."

"I'm fine, but I'm coming over."

"Now?"

"Yeah. I'm leaving as soon as we hang up," Mulder said.

"I'm not going to be home. I'm heading to a D and D game. After watching Earl Roy put you in a choke hold, I need a few hours without serial killers."

"You're kidding, right?" Mulder didn't want to act like a jerk, but this was important.

"You don't need me here." Gimble was scrambling to come up with a solution. "The Major knows you. I'll tell him you're coming. Just knock on the door and give him the code words when he asks."

"Are you sure? I don't want him coming after me with a mop." Mulder got the impression that the Major was even tougher than he looked.

"Wait five minutes. I'll call back if there's a problem," Gimble said. "Otherwise, you can come over."

"What did you tell him about last night?" Mulder didn't want to slip up and get Gimble in trouble.

"I told him that you're a crappy driver and you got us lost in the middle of nowhere."

"Got it. But shouldn't you tell him the truth? What if the sheriff's office calls?" Mulder asked, relieved that his own father was still out of town.

"I didn't think about that." Gimble was quiet for a moment. "I'll just unplug the phone and take it with me to the game."

"If I don't hear back, I'll leave in five." Mulder hung up.

"Where are you going?" Phoebe's voice came out of nowhere, and she startled him. Getting knocked out and thrown in a dog kennel had made him jumpy.

"I thought you were still asleep," he said.

She leaned against the doorjamb. "You didn't answer my question."

"I'm going to Gimble's house to talk to the Major. I think he might be able to help me find the other killer." He rubbed the back of his neck. "Do you want to come?"

She shook her head, tangled blond hair grazing her neck. "I'm going to call my parents. They're going to find out eventually. It's better if they hear it from me."

"That's probably a good idea." Not that he was doing it. "Can you ask them to not say anything? Just tell them my mom would be embarrassed to talk about it."

"Did you actually tell her?" Phoebe asked, shocked.

"That would be a *no*. My dad can deal with that when he gets home."

Gimble didn't call back, which gave Mulder the all clear. He hung out with Phoebe until she was ready to call her parents.

"Wish me luck," she said on his way out.

He smiled at her. "Luck."

For both of us.

Mulder rang the doorbell and waited. The Major was expecting him, but navigating the man's rocky mental terrain without Gimble there to help him still felt strange.

"Code words?" the Major asked from the other side of the door.

"Agent of Chaos." The name gave Mulder the creeps now.

The sound of five dead bolts unlocking one at a time was a relief.

The Major cracked the door open and peeked out. "Get in here before *they* see you." He ushered Mulder inside.

Mulder wondered if by *they* he meant the *government* or the *aliens*.

"Thanks for letting me come over, sir."

"So what's on your mind, airman? Gary said you need my help." He walked into the living room. The television was on, set to a local news channel. "I assume the conversation we're about to have is classified?"

"Absolutely." Mulder nodded and drifted toward the map on the Major's wall. "I wanted to take another look at all the information you've collected."

"Take a look, and I'll get us something to drink." The Major didn't have to ask him twice.

Mulder looked up at the newspaper articles and grainy photos, and the larger crime scene photographs Sergio had stolen from the coroner's office. He was instantly transfixed. The grisly photos drew him in, as if the images had their own gravitational pull. He had missed something the first time he stood in this spot. But that was *before* Earl Roy inadvertently revealed that he wasn't the only killer. He heard the Major banging around in the kitchen. Mulder peeked in and watched Gimble's dad remove the bicycle chain from the refrigerator door handles.

Mulder's mom had never recovered from losing Samantha, but she was functional—burnt casseroles and kitchen fires aside. But the Major wasn't burning dinner. Losing his wife had broken him.

Mulder went back to studying the crime scene photos and the map for clues, and the Major returned with two glass bottles of Perrier sparkling water.

Who drinks bottled water? Isn't that a European thing?

He handed Mulder a bottle. "Check the seal," the Major said, doing the same. "You can never be too careful."

Mulder twisted it open and took a sip, his attention still focused on the wall.

"Are you in danger, son? Because you've got the look of a man obsessed."

Mulder took a deep breath. "My sister disappeared when I was twelve. I was in the room with her, but I blacked out or something, and I don't remember anything." He wasn't sure why he chose that moment to tell the Major, but he wanted Gimble's dad to understand why this was so important to him.

"Sounds like a mind wipe. Advanced technology. Too advanced to be man-made. I was wiped back in 1973."

"What happened?" Mulder was intrigued. Worst-case scenario, he could use the story for an English assignment.

The Major walked to the end of the room, where the subject matter on the wall shifted from adult murder victims to aliens. Images of UFOs and crop circles were taped beside magazine pages that featured interviews with scientists and alien "abductees."

He touched a photo of himself standing next to a sign with the name of an air force base on it. "In October 1973, I was stationed at El Rico Air Force Base. It was a terrible assignment, on a nothing base, with civilian G-men wandering around, 'assessing' our performance. That was the story handed down to us, anyway."

"Do you know what they were evaluating?"

The Major snorted. "Nothing. It was a cover story to keep officers like me out of their hair, while they screwed around in one of our hangars." He frowned and his face clouded over. "I didn't realize it back then, but the forces of Chaos and Law were in the middle of a dogfight right under our noses."

He raked his fingers back and forth over his scalp, as if it was itching like crazy. "I should've known that every damn word my commanding officer was telling me was a lie. He was in on the whole operation. And the cover-up."

"Do you know what they were hiding?"

The Major rushed to the bookshelves. "I didn't at the time, but I figured it out later. My team had just completed a recon operation, and it hadn't gone well. It was late, but I couldn't sleep, so I decided to walk it off." He flipped over the seat cushion of the recliner and slid a green paperback out from underneath it.

Another copy of *Stormbringer*. Seeing the name of the fictional sword that formed the basis for Earl Roy's delusions sent bile crawling up Mulder's throat.

The Major clutched the book against his chest like a security blanket. "I headed out to the hangar, the one that everyone on base was supposed to steer clear of, and I circled around to the back of the building." He rubbed a hand over his face. "What I saw . . . I didn't remember it for a long time. Then the mind wipe wore off enough for me to piece the memory together. The Cigarette

Smoking Man's face came back to me first. He was standing behind the hangar. I knew he was a government man. The tie and long black coat gave him away. He was holding a cigarette, waiting while a bunch of other suits went in. He took a folded American flag from one of them and followed the group inside."

"Okay?" Mulder wasn't sure where this was going.

"I snuck in behind them and stayed against the back wall, in the shadows. The men walked toward the center of the hangar and the far end of the building opened up, and a bright light shined in. The Cigarette Smoking Man stepped forward and set the flag down like an offering. . . ."

Mulder was so wrapped up in the story that he encouraged the Major to keep talking. "To who?"

"Not to *who* . . . to *what*." The Major clutched the paperback tighter. "I wouldn't have believed it if I hadn't seen it with my own eyes. It was a living, breathing alien. The creature's body was shaped like a human's, but its skin was gray and wrinkled, and its head was too big for its body. But the alien's eyes were what scared me. It had gigantic bug eyes, and they were black like a television screen that was turned off."

"Maybe it was a prank? A guy in a costume or something?" Mulder offered, but a part of him wanted to believe the story.

"It was one of *them*. Just one." The Major's eyes darted around the room. "And the Cigarette Smoking Man . . . he was talking to it."

Mulder stared at Gimble's dad, speechless.

"That's it." The Major sounded defeated. "I got scared, and I took off so they wouldn't catch me."

That seemed like plenty to Mulder.

"I know what I saw." The Major sounded like the scout leader from the episode of *Project U.F.O.* He walked over to the recliner and straightened the seat cushion before he sat down. "But no one believed me, and she paid the price."

His wife.

A heavy silence fell over the room.

The weatherman on TV chattered in the background. ". . . a high of fifty-seven degrees, with a ten percent chance of rain."

Then a woman cut in. "Thank you, Tom. And now the latest on Earl Roy Propps, the man the press is calling the Lullaby Killer. If you missed our coverage this morning, thirty-two-year-old Earl Roy Propps of Craiger, Maryland, was apprehended by the Anne Arundel County Sheriff's Department late last night." Footage of the dilapidated house appeared on the TV screen. It looked even more menacing in the early morning light.

"After receiving an anonymous tip, the sheriff's department arrived at the Propps residence, and sources told us they found Earl Roy Propps in the basement with two hostages—eight-year-old Sarah Lowe, who disappeared from her home five nights ago, and a teenage boy whose name has not been released. Deputies recovered numerous weapons from the house. The Lullaby Killer struck fear in the hearts of parents in the metro area as images like these surfaced."

Gimble would definitely have to tell the Major now.

A photo of the magpie with arrows sticking out of its body filled the screen, and the newscaster continued, "While the sheriff's department refused to speculate, the bird found with Billy Christian—another one of Propps's young victims—clearly signifies the occult."

"Tell the truth, damn it!" the Major shouted at the TV set. "The aliens took those kids. This Earl Roy person is a pawn in the government's game."

Mulder couldn't tell the Major that Earl Roy Propps had tried to kill him.

"WJLA News has just received new information related to the case," the newscaster said. "Brian North is live on the scene at Rock Creek Cemetery."

"What do you think they're up to now?" the Major asked.

Mulder shook his head. "I'm not sure."

The newscast cut to the field reporter standing at the top of the hill that overlooked the mausoleums. "This is Brian North, and I'm here at Rock Creek Cemetery, where another tragedy is rapidly unfolding. The Lullaby Killer is behind bars, but he still managed to leave another victim. The body of eight-year-old Daniel Tyler was discovered this morning. Tyler disappeared from his home in Cookstown, Virginia, six months ago. According to the FBI, the

Lullaby Killer left his calling card with Daniel's body—a magpie pierced with eight arrows. Now we are all asking the same question: Did Earl Roy Propps leave behind the bodies of other victims?"

The reporter glanced over his shoulder at the FBI agents at the scene, his expression solemn. "We don't have an answer yet, but we can take solace in the fact that a serial killer is off the streets."

"The FBI will figure it out," Mulder said under his breath. "They can't be that stupid."

The Major clamped a hand on his shoulder. "Son, I just told you that someone from the American government made contact with an alien on a US military base. Who knows how many more little gray men the bastards are hiding? And you're asking if FBI agents are stupid?"

"You don't understand. . . ." Mulder rubbed his eyes. The lack of sleep was catching up to him. He took a deep breath and started again. "There's another killer out there—the person who gave Earl Roy Propps the bones. Earl Roy has a serious aversion to blood, like a phobia. He can't stand the sight of it. A guy like that couldn't have committed those types of murders."

The Major seemed suspicious. "I didn't hear about that on the news. Where did you get your information?"

Mulder couldn't tell the Major the truth without getting Gimble in trouble.

"Intel," Mulder said, thinking fast. "You've got your sources and I've got mine."

The Major pursed his lips, studying him. "Good work, airman. Continue."

"Earl Roy left the chaos symbol with Billy Christian's and Daniel Tyler's bodies. I'm thinking maybe he's Chaos and the other killer is Law? Did the police find any bone arrows left with the adult victims?"

The Major snorted. "No. But that doesn't mean his symbol wasn't there. The police department is full of fools, just like the Federal Bureau of Idiots. Law left his name at every crime scene."

For a second, Mulder wasn't sure if he'd heard him correctly.

"You don't believe me?" The Major sounded amused.

Mulder realized his mouth was hanging open. "No. I—"

"I'm used to people doubting me. Not everyone wants to see the truth." He marched over to what Mulder was beginning to think of as the murder wall. "Do you want to see what I'm talking about, airman?"

"Yes, sir."

The Major pointed at an enlarged version of the article about the dead madam, who had been pimping out teenage girls. "Victim number one. Her body was discovered at oh-eight hundred. There." He pointed at the dumpster. "Notice anything unusual in the photograph?"

Mulder squinted, concentrating. "Umm . . . her shoe is on the ground? Maybe it fell off during the struggle?"

"This will be your last black op if you can't do better than that." The Major rapped his knuckles against the wall. "I didn't ask what you *thought*. I asked what you *saw*."

"A dumpster in an alley and a woman's high-heeled shoe. Graffiti and a liquor store sign."

"You sure that's graffiti?"

Suddenly, Mulder saw it—a lone arrow pointing up, spray-painted above the dumpster.

"How about this one?" The Major moved on to a glossy black-and-white photograph of the drug-dealing psychiatrist's bedroom.

"Did Sergio get you this picture, too?"

"Sergio is a jack-of-all-trades," the Major said with pride. "The CIA wanted him, but Sergio turned them down."

I bet, Mulder thought.

The Major tapped on the photo. "Do you see it?"

Mulder searched for an arrow in the image. His eyes stopped on the nightstand. The pills the psychiatrist had taken—or, more likely, that someone had forced him to take—were scattered across the top of the nightstand, between empty prescription bottles.

Now that he knew what to look for, he saw it—a straight arrow formed by some of the pills. "I can't believe the cops missed this."

The Major shrugged. "They weren't looking for it. People see what they want to see. Or what the government tells them to."

Mulder was beginning to agree with him.

"And that's how they keep the aliens a secret," the Major added.

If the Major stopped tossing around the word *alien*, he would seem pretty brilliant.

"Right," Mulder said, zeroing in on the photograph of the slumlord hanging from the ceiling fan with a rope around his neck. "There it is." He pointed at a sheet of paper on the floor next to a fast-food bag and a pile of clothes. "On the flyer."

The instructions on the notice read: IF EVICTED, LEAVE APART-MENT KEYS IN THIS LOCKBOX.

A vertical arrow pointed at the top of the page, where a strip of masking tape ran along the edge.

"The police probably thought the guy was about to put *up* the notice," the Major explained. "But someone could've easily taken it down and left it inside the apartment."

"It isn't over." Mulder felt the weight of his words and what they really meant.

"Not even close." Gimble's dad glanced over his shoulder and lowered his voice. "The aliens won't stop until they get what they want."

"And what *is* that exactly?"

The Major looked down at the worn paperback in his hand. "I have my theories, but only one person knows for sure. The man I saw talking to one of them."

The Cigarette Smoking Man from El Rico Air Force Base—if the man was more than a figment of the Major's imagination.

"I've gotta go, sir." Mulder headed for the door. "The other killer is still out there."

"I don't know where you got your intel, airman, but this is too big for you to take on alone."

The scene in Earl Roy's basement proved that Mulder couldn't even handle the Eternal Champion's sidekick. What if he came up against the other killer—the "real" Eternal Champion? "Then I'll get help. Maybe I should talk to someone at the FBI?"

The Major followed him to the door. "Did you listen to a word I said? The FBI can't help anyone, and they might be working with the aliens. What if they report you?"

"I'll have to risk it . . . for my sister. I don't know if Earl Roy is the person who took her, but I still have to try." Mulder knew that if it was Earl Roy, the odds of Samantha being alive were slim to zero.

Mulder held out his hand. "Thanks for your help, sir." They shook hands, and Mulder held on for an extra second. He looked the Major in the eye. "Sir, I just want to say that I'm sorry about what happened to your wife."

The Major nodded and was silent for a moment. Then he looked up. "There's something I need to give you."

"That's okay—" Mulder didn't need another copy of *Stormbringer*.

"Don't argue with a superior officer unless you want to get your tail handed to you." The Major scribbled on a scrap of paper and handed it to Mulder. "If you get in over your head, call that number. Sergio will answer. It's a secure line, but he'll still ask you for the code words—"

"Agent of Chaos?" Mulder wasn't sure how a guy who carried out his top secret missions from his mom's basement could help, but he appreciated the gesture. "Thanks again, sir. And the next time I come by, I really do want to check out that telescope."

"Anytime, airman." The Major unlocked the dead bolts and reached for the knob. "But be careful. If you start putting the puzzle together, the FBI will start paying attention. You can't trust them."

Mulder didn't know much about the FBI.

But I have to trust someone.

CHAPTER 24

Mulder Residence
8:42 P.M.

Mulder had been holed up in his bedroom for hours. After his conversation with the Major, he drove straight home and ransacked his room, searching for every single secondhand psychology textbook he'd brought from home. Phoebe helped, even though she wasn't sure what he was trying to find. He wasn't sure himself.

The Meaning of Murder was his go-to when it came to anything related to the topic. The book referenced personality disorders and psychological conditions that suddenly felt critical for him to understand.

The information in one of those books could hold the answer to catching Law—the Eternal Champion.

Mulder was diving into an abnormal psychology text to learn more about the signs of a split personality when the apartment door slammed.

For a split second, he forgot that Earl Roy was in police custody.

"Mulder?" his father shouted from the living room. "Mulder? Where the hell are you?"

"He sounds really pissed," Phoebe whispered. "And when did he start calling you that?"

"It's a long story."

Interacting with his dad sucked on a normal day, but after being locked in a dog kennel by a delusional psychopath, he wasn't in the mood. Mulder dropped the textbook on his bed and prepared to storm out of the room when his door flew open instead. It banged against the wall so hard that it rebounded and almost hit his dad in the face.

"Where the hell have you been?" The rage in his dad's eyes took him by surprise.

"I've been here all night." Mulder picked up the psych book. He had never seen his father this angry. "Reading and hanging out with Phoebe."

Phoebe waved.

"I thought you weren't coming home for three more days."

His dad's eyes narrowed, and he looked at Mulder with contempt. "I thought so, too, until I got a call from the FBI!"

Oops.

"Do you want to explain why you were in Craiger, Maryland, looking for a serial killer—who almost hacked you to pieces in his basement?" His father's voice rose.

"The guy was kidnapping and murdering kids. Someone had to find the missing little girl."

Mulder's dad jabbed his finger in the air. "Why did it have to be you?"

The question loomed.

"You know why," he fired back.

"This obsession of yours is dangerous. And it ends here."

Mulder leaped off the bed. "You don't get to decide when it *ends*. It won't end for me until I find my sister."

Phoebe stared at her hands folded in her lap. Mulder wished she didn't have to hear this.

His dad slumped against the wall. "She's gone. You can't save her. You and your mother need to let this go."

His stomach caved in like his father had punched him, and every muscle in his body tightened. "I'll find out what happened to her."

Mulder's dad seemed to shrink before his eyes. He had already given up on the possibility of finding Samantha. Just like he gave up on his marriage and his relationship with his son. Samantha wasn't the only one who had disappeared that night almost five and a half years ago. His father had vanished, too.

Except he had a choice.

Maybe Mulder's father blamed him for blacking out and not saving his sister.

"Do you want to talk about what happened in that man's house?"

Mulder looked at his dad, disgusted. "With you? No thanks."

"Fine. But the FBI wants you to come in tomorrow afternoon. They have questions. And we're *not* telling your mother about this. You're lucky they called me first." Bill Mulder gave Phoebe a stern look to make sure she knew that his directive applied to her as well. He stormed out of the room, and his office door slammed a moment later.

"Are you okay?" Phoebe asked.

"Yeah." He picked up a stack of books and his notes. "But I want to finish this before I talk to the FBI."

"What is it you're finishing exactly?" she asked.

"I'm not sure yet." It was the truth.

Phoebe nodded. "Then finish it and find out."

Mulder turned his attention back to the books. He opened his copy of *Stormbringer* and tried to imagine what kind of man would take on the persona of "Law"—someone who chooses the sinners and thinks he has the right to act as judge and jury. A man who is dependent on the power he believes he gets from a demonic sword.

He made a list of everything he knew about Earl Roy Propps and the elaborate fantasy world he'd created based on Michael

Moorcock's series—in which Earl Roy was the companion and protector of the Eternal Champion.

Mulder outlined the chronology, including the eight-day period the children were drugged and held captive in the killer's basement, the detailed rituals Earl Roy engaged in to prepare them for the end, and the way he arranged their bodies after he poisoned them. His psych textbooks confirmed what he already knew—Earl Roy suffered from delusions and hallucinations, like hearing the "sword" talk to him and seeing it glow inside the kids.

Between the brief time he'd spent with Earl Roy and the snippets of information that had been released about the man, it was clear that Earl Roy Propps was no genius. He'd dropped out of high school at fifteen and, even as a mechanic, had spent more time doing oil changes than actually fixing cars. Then he moved on to unloading plants at a nursery. A guy like that couldn't stage a drug overdose or a suicide convincing enough to fool the police.

There was also the complicated sheepshank knot used in the slumlord's hanging. It had only taken the deputy a few seconds to untie the ropes around Mulder's wrists. A knot like a sheepshank would've required more time.

But Earl Roy's admissions while he was alone with Mulder and his aversion to blood were the real proof.

Mulder reached for a fresh legal pad and started writing. He wrote until his hand was numb and his vision blurred. He didn't stop writing when Phoebe fell asleep just after three in the morning, or when his father banged on the door to tell him Gimble was in the living room—or when his friend came in and sat on the floor across from him. Mulder didn't stop writing until he put a period after the last sentence.

"Mulder." His father burst into the room. "We have to leave. Now."

He ignored his dad and flipped to the front of the legal pad.

"Do you mind if I catch a ride with you, Mr. Mulder?" Gimble asked. He was wearing a baggy suit and a striped tie that was too long. "I'm supposed to go in and give a statement, too. But my dad doesn't really drive . . . or leave the house." Gimble held up a folded piece of paper. "He gave me a note."

"Sure." Bill Mulder looked down at Gimble with pity.

"I'm coming, too," Phoebe said. "My parents won't be here until this afternoon, so I have nothing else to do."

"Did the FBI call them?" Mulder's dad asked.

"Yeah. They're taking me to the interview tomorrow." She grabbed her bag. "Just give me a minute to change."

Bill Mulder turned his attention to his son's room, eyeing the books and papers strewn across the floor.

Mulder stood next to Gimble. "How did the Major take it when you told him?"

Gimble shook his head. "I never got around to it. The FBI showed up at my house because they couldn't get in touch with my dad over the phone. Especially after I left it at my dungeon master's house."

Mulder's father opened his closet. "Where's your suit?" he asked, riffling through the hanging clothes.

"I'll find it myself," Mulder snapped, but his dad ignored him. Whatever. There was nothing interesting in there anyway, and he wanted to hear the rest of Gimble's story.

"Did the Major flip?" he asked.

Gimble shrugged. "Pretty much. He wouldn't let them in the house, so they had to stand on the front steps to talk to him. But it was worse after they left. He didn't believe we were at Earl Roy's place. He thinks they made up the whole story. He wanted to drive to Canada so they couldn't interview me."

"That sucks." Mulder felt bad for his friend, and the FBI agents who showed up at the Major's door.

"Tell me about it. He thinks the aliens are going to abduct me from the FBI headquarters."

Mulder's father marched over to the bed and tossed down a stack of clothes, still on the hangers. Navy blazer, white dress shirt, gray slacks, and a light-blue-and-navy tie that definitely didn't belong to Mulder. His dad was probably slipping preppy Georgetown University–approved clothing into his closet.

"Get changed. Unless you would rather wait for the FBI to show up on our doorstep, too?" His dad stormed out and Gimble followed, stifling a smile.

Mulder changed his clothes and grabbed the legal pad. This was his chance to speak with a real FBI agent—someone with the power to launch an investigation and hunt down a serial killer. He just needed to find one person to listen.

To believe.

CHAPTER 25

The Hoover Building dominated Pennsylvania Avenue between 9th Street and 10th Street, like a concrete fortress. It wasn't the only massive building downtown, but the fact that the FBI and its subdivisions were the only occupants made a formidable impression.

When Mulder and his friends entered the building with his dad, the FBI seal on the wall immediately grabbed Gimble's attention. Mulder had seen it before in photos, but it was a lot cooler to see the seal from inside the FBI building. In the center of a blue circle, two laurel branches flanked a red-and-white-striped shield, with a scale above it and a white scroll below it. The image was surrounded with gold stars, and a blue border with block lettering on it.

Everyone stared, except his father, who managed to seem bored and annoyed at the same time.

Gimble pulled at his tie. "I want to read what it says."

But Bill Mulder wasn't in the mood for sightseeing. Gimble had barely taken a step when he said, "Department of Justice. Federal Bureau of Investigation. Now, let's check in or you'll be late."

He strode past them to the security desk.

Phoebe tightened her pigtails with a fierce look in her eye, as if she was adjusting her armor, then marched over to the seal. Mulder and Gimble followed.

When they caught up with her at the wall, she turned to Mulder. "Remember all the times I lectured you about being too hard on your dad? I feel bad saying this, but you were right. He is a jerk."

Mulder nudged her shoulder. "I think he has a chronic condition that prevents him from acting like a human being for longer than ten minutes at a time."

"Maybe he's a cyborg?" Gimble grinned, on the verge of cracking up at his own joke.

"He'd have a higher likability quotient," Mulder said, watching as his dad turned away from the desk and looked around for them. Bill Mulder shook his head and scowled when he realized they had ignored his pointless order. Mulder had seen that expression on his dad's face plenty of times, and it always bothered him.

Until today.

Mulder ushered Gimble and Phoebe back to the desk where his father was waiting. He ignored his son and continued making small talk with the man behind the desk until an agent arrived to escort them up to the fifth floor.

When everyone got off the elevator, Mulder and his friends followed the adults, who were engaged in a boring conversation about the State Department. Mulder studied the framed photos on the walls as he walked down the hallway. Most of them were old black-and-white photos of DC—the White House and the Capitol Building, the Lincoln Memorial and the view of the Reflecting Pool, and the previous FBI building.

The agent led them into a large office suite with a waiting area. A tall man wearing round wire glasses and a conservative navy suit stood at the desk, talking to the woman behind it. Her lipstick was a dark shade of red, like Mulder's mom used to wear when his father took her somewhere special—back when she still had special places to go.

"I'm scheduled for an interview with Agent Barnes," the man in the glasses told her. He kept adjusting his tie, tightening it and then loosening it again, as if he wasn't used to wearing one.

It made Mulder less self-conscious about all the tie readjusting he'd been doing.

The woman with the red lipstick handed him his driver's license. "Relax. If you're meeting with Agent Barnes, the bureau is interested in you."

"I hope you're right," he confided, adjusting his tie again. "I'm graduating in May, and this is the first job that has interested me."

Phoebe kicked Mulder's foot just hard enough to get his attention. "Check out the posters," she whispered.

Empty eyes and cold expressions stared at them from the WANTED BY THE FBI posters plastered on the walls. Mulder turned in a circle, examining the faces. Some were familiar—John Wayne Gacy, the Killer Clown, who had finally been caught last year after slaughtering thirty-three teenage boys in Illinois; David Berkowitz, Son of Sam; Edward Wayne Edwards, a convicted serial killer who had started killing again after he was paroled. Some of the posters had the word CAPTURED stamped across them in red.

"This room is gonna give me nightmares," Gimble whispered.

Not Mulder.

The images sent pinpricks up the back of his neck and a rush of adrenaline pumping through his veins. The thought of catching monsters like the ones pictured on the posters made him think about Samantha, Billy, and Sarah. Catching those monsters mattered.

"It will only be a minute," said the young agent who had escorted them upstairs.

"Right," Mulder's dad snapped, the moment the agent was out of earshot. He barely got the words out before a door opened and another agent came out to greet them.

"Special Agent John Douglas, from the FBI's Behavioral

Science Unit." He extended his hand to Bill Mulder, who gave it a quick shake.

"William Mulder. I'm with the State Department. Someone from your office called and asked me to bring in my son."

Agent Douglas had a hardscrabble look about him that Mulder liked.

"I'm actually scheduled to meet with Gary Winchester—"

"That's me." Gimble stepped forward.

"Nice to meet you," Agent Douglas said to Gimble, before continuing his conversation with Mulder's father. "Special Agent Ressler will be out in a minute. He'll be conducting the interview with your son."

Mulder's dad sighed, annoyed by the delay.

Agent Douglas ignored him. "So where's your father, Gary? I spoke with him on the phone briefly after the other agents spoke to him at your house."

"Oh. He doesn't leave the house," Gimble said, as if it was completely normal. "He told me to give you this." He handed Agent Douglas a sheet of paper folded into a perfect square.

The FBI agent raised an eyebrow and opened it. "'I, Major William Wyatt Winchester, retired major of the 128th Recon Squadron of the United States Air Force, grant the United States Federal Bureau of Investigation permission to interview my son, Gary William Winchester, on April 4, 1979. I do not grant permission for FBI agents, or other persons employed by the United States government, to ask my son questions about myself, or my work as a civilian. Sincerely, Major William Wyatt Winchester, USAF.'"

Agent Douglas scratched his head and examined the note. "I've never seen anything quite like this."

Gimble shrugged. "Yeah. My dad likes to do his own thing."

"We don't usually accept legal documents without a notary seal, or ones written in highlighter."

"I told him that, but he couldn't find a pen," he explained.

"Right." Agent Douglas gestured for Gimble to follow him as he opened the door. "Why don't we go ahead and get started, Gary?"

Before the door closed, Mulder heard his friend say, "By the way, everyone calls me Gimble."

"You didn't tell me your best friend's father had a screw loose," Mulder's dad said.

Phoebe shot him a dirty look.

But as far as Mulder was concerned, that was letting him off too easy. "Don't talk about the Major like that. He's a good man. I don't care what you think."

His father's face turned red. "What did you just say to me?"

Mulder heard the door close behind him and turned to find another FBI agent watching them.

"Special Agent Robert Ressler." The agent approached Bill Mulder and extended his hand. "I'm with the Behavioral Science Unit."

Mulder's father introduced himself, and Ressler turned to Mulder. "Fox, right?" Agent Ressler's sleeves were rolled up, and his button-down shirt was wrinkled, as if he'd slept in it.

"You can call me Mulder, and this my friend Phoebe Larson."

Phoebe smiled. "Nice to meet you."

"I think we have an appointment tomorrow, Miss Larson," Agent Ressler said.

"Then I guess I'll see you again tomorrow," she said.

Mulder's dad cleared his throat and gestured at the open door behind the agent. "Let's get this over with."

Agent Ressler held up his hand. "I'd prefer to speak to your son alone, if that's all right with you? There's a great coffee shop across the street. Best chocolate cream pie I've ever tasted."

Bill Mulder opened his mouth to argue, but Ressler kept talking. "I bet the State Department has a smart guy like you working around the clock."

"I *was* on a business trip when your office called me," Mulder's father grumbled. "I flew in last night."

Ressler offered a sympathetic nod. "So we're both overworked. Go ahead and take a break. Have a slice of pie."

"Are you all right with going in alone?" Mulder's dad asked him.

"Yeah." A week ago Mulder would've cared about the fact that his father was ditching him, during an interview about his son being held captive by a serial killer, to eat pie. Now he saw his dad for what he was—a coward who gave up on his family.

"I'll wait here," Phoebe said, planting herself in a vinyl chair. "For moral support."

"I'll run F—" Ressler caught himself. "Mulder and Phoebe across the street to you when we finish." He walked Bill Mulder to the hallway before the man changed his mind.

Ressler returned and ushered Mulder toward the door to the back offices. Mulder glanced over his shoulder to nod at Phoebe, and she gave him a thumbs-up.

"Can I get you a soda or a snack from the vending machine before we get started?" Agent Ressler asked as they walked down the hall.

"You got rid of my dad, so I'm good."

Ressler laughed. "My father isn't the easiest person to get along with, either."

By the time Mulder took a seat in front of Agent Ressler's desk, he felt comfortable enough to walk the agent through what they had pieced together and the events that had taken place at Earl Roy's house. Ressler sat behind his desk taking notes, even though he was recording the conversation. He stopped Mulder whenever he had a question or needed clarification, but mostly he just listened.

When Mulder finally finished telling his story, he slumped in the leather armchair. "It feels like I just ran a marathon."

"What you did took guts. You saved Sarah Lowe's life and stopped a killer who murdered at least two children," Ressler said.

Mulder sat up straight. "You said 'at least.' Does that mean you think he killed even more kids? Ones you haven't found yet?"

Because that's what I think.

"Recovering Daniel Tyler's body proves something I was afraid of."

His throat went dry. "What?"

Ressler unwrapped a roll of antacids sitting on his desk, popped two in his mouth, and swallowed them. "That Earl Roy Propps didn't start murdering kids five *days* ago. He's been doing this for a long time."

Something clicked in Mulder's mind. "Did you find the bikes in the backyard? Did they belong to other kids? Earl Roy had a bike for Sarah. He said it was a gift. I thought maybe the other bikes were gifts, too."

"We found the bikes," Ressler said. "But we aren't sure who they belonged to yet."

"Then what made you think Billy Christian wasn't Earl Roy's first victim?"

"It's my job to catch killers like Earl Roy, and I've been doing it long enough to recognize when I'm dealing with an experienced serial killer." Agent Ressler pushed his chair away from the desk and stood up. "I shouldn't be telling you this, but you'll hear about it on the news tonight, if the media hasn't figured it out already." He leaned against the wall behind his desk. "We found a third child's body, in another mausoleum at Rock Creek Cemetery. So that makes four victims, now."

"How did you know where Earl Roy hid the bodies? Did you find something at his house? Like a list? Or did he tell you himself?"

Ressler sat down again and propped his elbows on the desk. "No. We didn't have anything that concrete. But leaving the bodies in mausoleums fit Earl Roy's profile."

"I'm not sure what you mean by his profile."

"It's not a term many people use outside of the BSU. A profile is a psychological description of a violent offender based on what we know about their crimes," Ressler explained. "It's like putting together a puzzle when you don't have all the pieces—or the picture on the box to help you. My job is to fill in the missing pieces— ideally, before a killer leaves a trail of victims."

Mulder sat on the edge of his chair, hanging on Ressler's every word. "So the profile helped you figure out where to look for the bodies?"

"Exactly. Earl Roy is what we call a ritualistic killer. He engages in specific rituals that have symbolic meaning to him." Ressler pushed up his sleeves. "For example, he killed Billy after eight days, and he planned to do the same thing with Sarah. He left a bird pierced with arrows that were arranged in the same pattern with each body—it all pointed to a killer who would dispose of the bodies in the same way, and leave them in similar locations."

"So you started searching crypts?" Mulder pictured Ressler and a bunch of FBI agents wandering around Rock Creek Cemetery with crowbars.

"I let the cadaver dogs do that part," Ressler explained. "They're trained to find human remains."

"In a cemetery? The whole place is full of human remains." It sounded like trying to find a needle in a skyscraper-sized haystack.

"I said the same thing the first time one of my instructors at the FBI Academy introduced the concept. But cadaver dogs are highly trained. Some only detect old remains, and other dogs, like the ones we took to Rock Creek Cemetery, are trained to detect odors related to certain stages of decomposition."

"I still don't get it," Mulder said.

"This won't sound very scientific, but we used cemetery records and the process of elimination. Since Earl Roy left Billy in an empty crypt, we assumed he would've done the same thing with his earlier victims. So we only searched mausoleums, not graves, and we eliminated the ones without any empty crypts. We started with the mausoleums closest to the one where Billy's body was found."

Once Mulder realized that FBI agents weren't being pulled through the graveyard while they clung to the leashes of a pack of bloodhounds, he was impressed by the scientific nature of it all. "How long did it take the dogs to find the right crypts?"

"A few hours. Daniel's body was in a mausoleum two plots away from the one where Billy's body was found, and the girl's remains were recovered from the mausoleum across from it."

"The other victim was a girl?" Mulder barely got the words out.

Ressler nodded. "She disappeared in 1972."

"You're sure? Could it have been 1973?" he asked, his pulse drumming.

"Normally, I would say maybe. Remains that old take longer to identify. But in this case, we were able to ID the victim because of surgical evidence. She had pins in her hip from orthopedic surgery after a car accident."

Mulder heard what Ressler was saying, but he felt detached from the words, as if they were meaningless. The girl's body they had recovered wasn't Samantha's. That much had registered. But if Earl Roy had been killing kids as far back as 1972, his sister could've been one of them.

"What about 1973?" Mulder blurted out. "Do you know where Earl Roy was, or what he was doing? I'm asking because my sister, Samantha, was kidnapped in 1973, on November 27, from our house in Chilmark, Massachusetts. She was in the living room and the power went out. When it came back on, she was gone and the front door was left open, the same way it happened with the other kids."

"And you were there," Ressler said. It wasn't a question.

"Yeah. But I blacked out and I don't remember anything." Mulder looked Agent Ressler in the eyes. "Do you think Earl Roy Propps took my sister?"

Ressler turned off the tape recorder. "Officially? I don't know. The truth? It's possible."

"Were you involved with the investigation?"

"No. But I asked around after I read the write-up about your background."

"And?" Mulder's heartbeat pounded in his ears.

"No evidence was recovered, and there were never any suspects or any leads." Ressler shook his head. "I'm sorry. I really wish I had more to tell you."

Mulder nodded. The truth felt heavy and cold, like wearing a wet coat outside when it was freezing. He couldn't handle feeling this way for the rest of his life. Whoever took his sister must have left a trace—one tiny bread crumb for him to follow.

Somewhere.

Agent Ressler turned the tape recorder back on. "Nothing can make up for what you've lost, but you saved a girl's life. And you saved the lives of all the kids Earl Roy would've hurt if he was still free."

Ressler's acknowledgment didn't give Mulder any peace. The Eternal Champion was still out there. "I didn't do enough. Earl Roy didn't do this alone."

"What are you talking about?"

"I tried to tell the sheriff, but he wouldn't listen. There's a second killer. The person who gave Earl Roy the bones."

Ressler picked up his pen. "Did you see this person?"

"No."

"Then what makes you think there's another killer?"

"Earl Roy didn't just dig up old bones to make those arrows, but I'm guessing you already know that. The bones came from adult murder victims, and removing the bones themselves took some work—chopping-off-hands kind of work."

"Did Earl Roy tell you about that?" Ressler frowned and shook his head, disgusted.

Mulder wasn't about to tell Agent Ressler that he got the information by sneaking around the police station and looking at photos the Major's "source," Sergio, had stolen from the morgue.

"That doesn't matter. What I'm trying to tell you is that Earl Roy couldn't have done any of that. He can't handle the sight of blood." Mulder rushed on. "When I was locked up in his basement, I cut my hand. When Earl Roy saw the blood, the guy went ballistic."

Ressler started writing.

"I'm talking about a full-blown panic attack from a little blood smeared on the floor."

Mulder held up his hand so Ressler could see his palm. "That's the cut."

It was so small that Ressler had to lean over his desk to take a closer look.

"But Earl Roy crawled away from me like I had severed an artery. And he begged me—his *prisoner*—not to come near him. That's the reason he poisoned the kids. No blood. How could a guy like that hack up a body?"

"He couldn't," Ressler confirmed. "What you're describing is a called hemophobia. And you deduced there was a second killer based on the connection between the bones and Earl Roy's hemophobia?"

"Earl Roy also told me there was another killer," Mulder said. "In a delusional sort of way."

"I'm not sure I follow."

"He's obsessed with this fantasy series about the Eternal Champion, a character who fights to restore the balance between Chaos and Law. It's pretty complicated."

Ressler nodded. "We know about the books and the Eternal Champion. Propps hasn't stopped talking about them."

"He wouldn't shut up about it with me, either. He kept saying he was the Eternal Champion's protector. But it didn't click until I saw his reaction to the blood."

Agent Ressler leaned back in his chair, studying him.

Mulder recognized that look. "You don't believe me, either."

"Actually, I do." Ressler opened a folder and thumbed through the papers inside. "I witnessed Earl Roy's hemophobia firsthand."

"How?"

"When I spoke to the sheriff, he told me that you were in shock, and I should wait a few days before I interviewed you. He said you thought there was another killer because Earl Roy was terrified of blood. He didn't take any of it seriously."

"But you did?" Mulder asked.

"I can't take the credit. I mentioned the conversation to Agent Douglas, and he decided to conduct an experiment. He tossed a crime scene photo on the table when we questioned Earl Roy."

"What happened?" Mulder tried to picture the scenario.

"He almost dislocated his shoulder trying to climb under the table to get away from the photograph. Not many people would've put this all together, Mulder. If you were older, I'd hire you." Ressler didn't sound like he was making fun of him.

"Wait. Then you believe there's another serial killer?" He stared at him in shock.

Ressler dodged the question by asking one himself. "When you were alone with Earl Roy, did he mention his brother?"

The word hit Mulder like a brick. "He has a brother?"

"Montgomery Propps. He's three years older than Earl Roy, and we suspect he was either directly involved in Earl Roy's crimes or he was at least aware of them. The fact that he didn't show up for work the morning after Earl Roy was arrested makes both scenarios more likely."

Mulder put the legal pad with his notes on Ressler's desk and pushed it toward him. "I don't know if this will help."

Ressler picked it up and skimmed the pages. "You wrote this?"

"Yeah. I stayed up all night working on it."

"These aren't notes, Fox. This is a profile of Montgomery Propps." He stared at Mulder, stunned. "And it *will* help. Sometimes profiles help us identify violent offenders, but we also use them to locate offenders faster. I need to show this to Agent Douglas, and then get it to our team at the BSU. Thank you."

Agent Ressler led Mulder back to the reception area, where Phoebe was reading a pamphlet. "Give me a few minutes," Ressler said. "And then I'll walk you over to the coffee shop to meet your dad."

"We'll be fine on our own," Mulder said. "It's right across the street."

"Stay put," Ressler ordered, still reading Mulder's notes as he pushed the office door open with his free hand.

The moment the door shut, Phoebe asked, "What just happened?"

It took Mulder a moment to respond. "I'm not really sure. But I think I just helped the FBI."

CHAPTER 26

Mulder spotted his father the minute he entered the coffee shop with Phoebe and Agent Ressler. His dad was parked at a table in the back of the restaurant, and from the plates on the table, it looked like he was on his second slice of pie.

His father stood up the moment he saw the FBI agent walking toward him. "How did it go? Was my son helpful?"

Ressler nodded. "Absolutely. Mulder is remarkably bright and his instincts are exceptional, two qualities we hold in high regard at the BSU."

Mulder's father tossed a few bills on the table. "Glad to hear it. But we have to get going. I'm needed at the office. The State Department took on a very ambitious project, and I'm the only person who understands the intricacies." The remark sounded like a sad attempt to point out that Mulder's exceptional genes were inherited from his even more exceptional father.

"We can't leave yet. Gimble is still meeting with Agent Douglas," Mulder said.

"They should be finished soon," Agent Ressler assured Bill Mulder. "Let me buy you a cup of coffee."

"I'll be over there with Phoebe." Mulder pointed to a booth across the aisle. He was done with his dad for today.

And tomorrow.

He grabbed Phoebe's hand, led her to a booth, and then slid into the seat.

"What did Agent Ressler say about what you wrote?" she asked the moment she sat down.

The waitress swooped in before Mulder could answer.

"Can I get you kids something?" she asked, slipping the pencil from behind her ear.

They hadn't looked at the menus tucked behind the napkin dispenser yet. But he just wanted to get rid of the woman so they could be alone. "I'll just have a slice of pie," he said.

"Me too," Phoebe said.

"What kind? We have apple, cherry, lemon, Boston cream—"

Mulder cut her off. "Sweet potato."

The waitress raised her eyebrows but wrote it down. "And for you?" she asked Phoebe.

"Chocolate?"

"Chocolate cream or chocolate silk?"

"Chocolate cream," Phoebe said quickly, sensing that Mulder was losing his patience. The waitress started to ask another question, and she added, "And two waters. Thank you so much."

When the waitress finally walked away, Phoebe folded her legs on the seat and got comfortable. "So what did Agent Ressler think about your notes?"

"I don't know. He seemed sort of . . . impressed. Ressler said the notes I gave him are called a profile."

"Your notes have a name?" Now she was impressed, too.

"Seems like it." A hint of a smile played on Mulder's lips. "From what Ressler told me, a profile is like a window into a violent offender's mind. The FBI uses them to hunt down serial killers like Earl Roy Propps."

Phoebe leaned back against the booth and tilted her head to the side, studying him. "You were only in his office for an hour and you already have the jargon down?"

Mulder shrugged, suddenly embarrassed. "It's not that big of a deal."

She looked across the table at him and their eyes locked. "You saved a girl's life, Fox. It doesn't get much bigger than that."

"Thanks." He had just wanted to stop a monster and protect that little girl, the way he hadn't been able to protect his sister. But he finally let himself feel proud of what he'd done.

The waitress came over and dropped off their pie. She forgot the waters.

Mulder shoved a forkful of pie in his mouth.

"If Agent Ressler was impressed with the profile, then he must've believed you when you told him about the second killer," Phoebe said.

Mulder leaned in. "Ressler already knew. One of the deputies told him about the way Earl Roy flipped out at the sight of blood. So Ressler set Earl Roy up and showed him a crime scene photo."

"And?" She was hanging on every word.

"Earl Roy tried to climb under the table and hide. Plus, Ressler thinks he knows who Earl Roy was working with. He has a brother. Montgomery Propps."

"And his brother is still out there somewhere?" She pushed away her plate, the pie untouched.

"Yeah. But Agent Ressler said the profile I wrote might help the FBI find him faster."

"It sounds like you're good at this. And maybe it's something you're interested in?"

The waitress came to the table again. "The two men in the booth over there paid your check."

Mulder's dad and Agent Ressler were out of their seats. His father gestured toward the front of the coffee shop.

"Looks like we're leaving," Phoebe said.

Mulder wasn't looking forward to going back to the apartment. He had nothing left to say to his dad—except that he wouldn't be attending Georgetown University in the fall.

"I'm glad we had a chance to meet, Fox Mulder." Agent Ressler extended his hand.

Mulder shook it. "Me too."

"Aren't you coming?" Phoebe asked Ressler.

"I'm heading back to Quantico, to the BSU." He looked at Mulder. "There's a profile I want to get over to my colleagues as soon as possible."

As Ressler turned to leave, Mulder realized he had another question. "Agent Ressler? What's a good major for someone who wants to join the FBI after they finish college?"

Ressler smiled. "Psychology."

"Political science and economics will carry you further, and Georgetown has top-notch programs in both," Mulder's dad couldn't resist mentioning.

"That's good to know," Mulder said. "But I'm not going to Georgetown."

Phoebe's mouth fell open.

Bill Mulder's nostrils flared and his jaw muscles twitched. "What did you say?"

Mulder ignored him and looked at the FBI agent. "And which school has the best psych program?"

"That's easy. Oxford."

"Thanks." He watched as Ressler pushed up his rolled sleeves and opened the door to leave.

Agent Ressler paused to say one more thing. "Come see me when you need a job in a few years."

CHAPTER 27

The window slid open, as if someone had greased it just for X. People wasted ridiculous amounts of money buying reinforced doors and high-tech dead bolts to protect their homes, but nine times out of ten they skimped on the windows—and any halfway decent criminal knew it.

He started to push the window up the rest of the way, and it got stuck.

X heard his father's voice in the back of his mind. "That's what you get for being such a know-it-all."

Guess his loser father was right for once in his life. It was a shame the man was buried too deep in the ground to enjoy it.

X's mouth stretched into a satisfied smile.

You never forget the first person you kill.

Two minutes and twelve seconds later, he returned the lock pick to his wallet and ducked under the window frame and into the room.

A flash of red caught his eye, and he noticed the poster on the back of the door.

Farrah Fawcett.

The kid had good taste.

He dusted off his pants and felt a twinge of . . . guilt? All right, maybe he felt a little sorry for the kid. It was hard for a boy to lose his father.

Unless you killed him yourself.

It was the kind of thing his boss would say.

He walked by the desk and flicked a model of the *Enterprise* from *Star Trek* hanging above it. "Sorry, kid." X watched it spin. "Your dad should've kept his mouth shut."

He slipped out of the bedroom and closed the door behind him, but not before he kissed two of his fingers and touched them to Farrah's lips. In the hallway, he heard the crackle of static, followed by a man's voice.

Time to go to work.

Halfway down the stairs, he caught a glimpse of his mark. This would be easier than he had expected.

"Sergio, can you hear me?" More static. "Staff Sergeant? Report."

"Sergio is *unavailable*," X said. "You sound like a real crackpot calling him on that thing. If only everyone knew how sane you are . . ."

The man dropped the microphone. But he recovered quickly and jumped to his feet. "Who the hell are you, and what are you doing in my house?"

X took off his blazer and draped it over the banister. "You don't remember me, Major Winchester? That hurts."

The Major studied X. "I don't know you, and I never forget a face."

"Unless we want you to." X walked toward the Major. "It seems like you're remembering a lot these days. Unfortunately, that's a problem." He slid a pair of black leather gloves out of his pocket and put them on. "And I'm a problem *solver.*"

The Major's eyes went wide. "You're one of *them.*" He took a step back. "What did you do to Sergio?"

"If I were you, I'd worry about yourself."

"Whatever they promised you, it's all lies," the Major stammered. "They want our planet. Are you just going to hand it over to them?"

X moved closer. "The world *is* a pretty messed-up place. . . ."

The Major held his hands out in front of him. "I have a son. He needs me. Just give me a little time to make sure he'll be all right."

"Gary, right?" X asked, measuring the Major's reaction. "Don't worry about him. He's a smart kid. We're already keeping an eye on him."

"Leave my boy alone, or I'll find you in hell." The Major's tone turned to ice. "That's a promise."

"You've got a lot of fight in you, Major Winchester. It's a shame you picked the wrong team."

"You don't have to do this." The Major tried to take another step back, but there was nowhere left to go.

"It's funny. . . . Your wife said exactly the same thing." X tilted his head to the side. "You think that's a coincidence?"

The Major's expression clouded over. "There are no coincidences."

He lunged at X, who pivoted to the side at the last possible moment. As the Major charged past him, X moved behind. In a rapid succession of movements, he reached over the Major's shoulder and grabbed his chin, then caught the back of the man's head with his other hand and jerked his hands in opposite directions. "I agree."

X felt the vertebrae crack, and he let the Major's body fall to the floor in a heap.

Now the real work began. X ripped the newspaper articles and photos of fake UFOs off the walls. He didn't have anything against the Major's amateur private investigator status, but he didn't have time to wade through all this crap. So it all had to go.

The basement was next. A heavy-duty cable and padlock secured the door. X should've brought along a pair of bolt cutters. The nice thing about conspiracy theorists who were anticipating an alien invasion was that they always had plenty of emergency supplies. And they kept them in the same spot in the kitchen as everybody else.

"The cupboard under the sink," X said as he bent down to open it. He picked up the red fire extinguisher and marched back to the basement door. He brought the base of the fire extinguisher down hard against the top of the lock.

Once.

Twice.

Three times—and it broke off.

X's boss wanted a specific file. Number 12179. "It will have 'El Rico Air Force Base' stamped on the front."

Easy enough.

The light switch at the top of the stairs had been removed, leaving the wiring exposed. With the basement door open, X could see well enough to navigate the stairs and locate the chain dangling from a bare bulb at the bottom. He pulled the chain, and a panel of fluorescent lights on the ceiling turned on one by one.

The entire room was full of cardboard file boxes stacked ten high. A commercial copy machine was wedged between stacks of green paperback books. X picked one up.

"*Stormbringer?* You were some kind of crazy, Major Winchester." He opened a file box and took out one of the cream-colored files.

#12179. EL RICO AFB.

X pulled out two more, then opened another box and checked those. Every folder was labeled the same way.

#12179. EL RICO AFB.

"You won this round, Major." He stopped in front of the wall across from the stairs.

The Major had written a message in huge black letters.

CAN YOU HANDLE THE TRUTH???

"You'll never find out," X said as he pulled the chain under the lightbulb and walked up the stairs.

X retrieved his blazer from where he'd left it draped over the banister and slipped it on. He strolled through the kitchen and stopped at the stove. From the interior pocket of his blazer, he pulled out the gift from the boss.

Nothing extravagant. Just practical.

A simple turn of a knob and the burner ignited. X leaned over with the Morley between his lips and lit the cigarette. One drag, and he headed to the back door. A halo of orange flames danced on the burner as he flicked the Morley onto the kitchen floor.

He was halfway down the alley behind the brownstones when

Major Winchester's kitchen exploded, taking the rest of the house with it in a matter of seconds.

X thought about the Major's kid. He was almost eighteen, and in DC, you only had to be seventeen to be legally declared an adult.

The kid will be okay.

But X did have one regret.

I should've taken the Enterprise.

CHAPTER 28

The black sedan with the tinted windows was parked across the street from Bill Mulder's apartment.

X knocked on the window, and the passenger door swung open.

"How did it go?" his boss asked without disturbing the Morley tucked in the corner of his mouth.

"I smoked my first cigarette," X said, leaning back against the seat.

"What did you think?"

"Not bad. But I see myself as more of a social smoker."

"Did you just make that up?" He took a long drag of his Morley, then pointed it at X. "And if you did, don't tell me. It sounds like the kind of garbage a guy in a white jumpsuit would say, and nobody should wear one of those except Elvis. And he's dead."

The Smoking Man was pissed off about something. X hoped it didn't have anything to do with him. The funnel of ash on his Morley grew with every drag. X didn't bother watching it. The ash wouldn't break off until the boss allowed it to fall.

"Did you get the file?" He exhaled, and smoke snaked toward X.

"Files. Plural. Boxes and boxes full of photocopies."

"I assume that was the reason for your fireworks show at the Winchester residence?"

"Yep."

"And the Major?"

"Broke his neck," X said. "I would've staged a natural death, but the guy was agitated. And there was no time."

"Don't make a habit of it." The Smoking Man blew out a long trail of smoke. "Anything to report on Fox Mulder?"

"Bill came home last night, and the two of them got into it." X shook his head. "The kid's dad really is a jerk."

"Bill means well. A son can't always understand his father's motivations. What were they arguing about?"

"The FBI had called Fox in to ask him some questions." A hint of a smile played on his lips. "The kid met with Agent Ressler from the BSU."

The boss nodded. "I know Bob. We went fishing once or twice.

The guy has no sea legs. He threw up the whole time." He tapped the edge of his cigarette on the ashtray and the funnel broke off in one piece, the way it always did. "How did Fox do with Ressler? On land, the man is tough."

"Ressler seemed impressed. He was surprised the kid pieced the case together on his own."

The Smoking Man rolled the cigarette between his fingers. "You followed Fox Mulder around for the past few days. How did he figure all this out?"

X sat with the question for a moment. "He definitely has good instincts. And he never discounted anyone without giving the person a chance. He even listened to Major Winchester."

"Fox Mulder is willing to believe."

The Cigarette Smoking Man kept staring at the building.

He took another drag. "Belief has its uses." Ⓧ

DON'T MISS
DANA SCULLY'S STORY

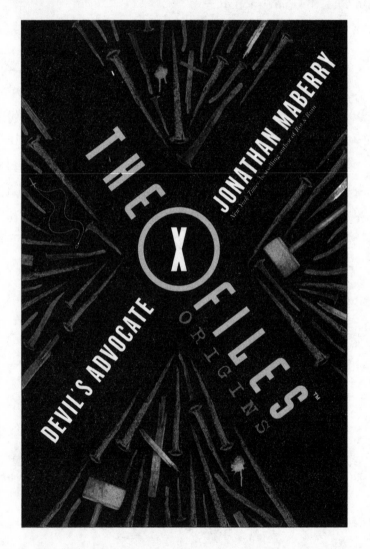

ACKNOWLEDGMENTS

Jonathan Maberry, my friend and fellow author: For coming up with the crazy idea to write about Fox Mulder as a teen, and for never abandoning it. If you hadn't talked me into writing the short story "Black Hole Son" about sixteen-year-old Fox Mulder for your anthology this book wouldn't exist. And no one else could've written Dana Scully's origin story. You're the real Agent of Chaos.

Jodi Reamer, my literary agent and the best in the business: For encouraging me to follow my crazy ideas down rabbit holes and helping me find my way out when I get lost.

Erin Stein, my publisher and editor at Imprint: For scoring me this gig and spending three days at my house outlining Mulder's story with me. But most of all, for letting me take risks in my novels.

Joshua Izzo and Nicole Spiegel at Twentieth Century Fox: For your excitement and support, and for helping us get this done so fast; and to the Team at IDW: for the amazing stories they're telling in the world of The X-Files Origins.

Chris Carter, creator of The X-Files: For creating Fox Mulder, one of the coolest and most iconic characters in television history, and for allowing me to write his origin story.

David Duchovny, the actor who brought Fox Mulder to life: For making us all Believe so completely.

Ellen Duda, senior designer at Imprint: For creating gorgeous cover art that captures the heart of the novel.

The "Believers" at Imprint: Natalie Sousa, Rhoda Belleza, and Nicole Otto. And to all the "Believers" at Macmillan: Jon Yaged, Angus Killick, Allison Verost, Molly Brouillette Ellis, Kelsey Marrujo, Lucy Del Priore, Kathryn Little, Johanna Kirby, Mariel Dawson, Robert Brown, Jeremy Ross, Caitlin Crocker, Grace Rosean, Jennifer Gonzalez and her incredible sales team, John Nora, Alexei Esikoff, and the eagle eyes of Valerie Shea and Christine Ma.

Writers House, my literary agency: For representing me and my literary works, with special thanks to Cecilia de la Campa and Alec Shane.

Dr. Thomas Sixbey, MD, and Dr. Edward Kurz, MD: For your unparalleled professional expertise regarding serial killers, the criminal mind, the FBI, and the BS. I can't thank you enough for spending hours answering my questions and texts. You are the coolest psychiatrists I've ever met, and this book would not be the same without you.

Lauren Oliver, my friend and fellow author: For knowing even more about serial killers than I do and for coming up with what shall forever be referred to as "the blood solution."

Sarah Weiss-Simpson, my assistant: For organizing my life so I have time to write. I couldn't make it through the day without you.

Chloe Palka, my social media manager: For your expertise, creativity, and ability to read my handwriting. You deserve your own X-File.

Erin Gross, Yvette Vasquez, and Ursula Uriarte, my friends and three of the smartest women I know: For your brilliance, patience, and friendship.

Benjamin Alderson, Caden Armstrong, Katie Bartow, Yvette Cervera, Bri Daniel, Andye Eppes, Jen Fisher, Vilma Gonzalez, Kristen Goodwin, Erin Gross, Sara Gundell, Ruthie Heard, Mara Jacobi, Taylor Knight, Hikari Loftus, Caden Sage, Evie Seo, Tracey Spiteri, Amber Sweeney, Natasha Tomic, Ursula Uriarte, Lauren Ward, Jenny Zemanek, and Heidi Zweifel—For being "Reckless" and offering me your insight, creativity, and support. I can't thank you enough or express how much it means to me.

Vania Stoyanova, my friend and photographer: For making me look cool in my author photo.

Lorissa Shepstone of Being Wicked, my graphic designer: For designing stunning graphics and swag, with little or no notice.

Eric Harbert and Nick Montano: For watching my back and being the best at what you do.

Alan Weinberger, my rheumatologist: For making sure I don't fall apart.

Librarians, teachers, booksellers, bloggers, bookstgrammers, booktubers, and my readers: For sticking with me when I venture into new territory, connecting with my characters, and spreading the word about The X-Files Origins novels and all my books. You are my tribe.

Mom, Dad, Celeste, John, Derek, Hannah, Hans, Alex, Sara, Erin, Temple, Ryley, and Sawyer, my parents, stepparents, siblings, sister-in-laws, nephew, and nieces: for your support and encouragement. I love you all.

Alex, Nick, and Stella: For believing in me, even when I don't believe in myself. I love you.